THE ROVER
ADVENTURES

Look out for Roddy Doyle's
other fantastic children's book:

WILDERNESS

Roddy Doyle

The Rover Adventures

SCHOLASTIC

Scholastic Children's Books
An imprint of Scholastic Ltd
Euston House, 24 Eversholt Street
London, NW1 1DB, UK
Registered office: Westfield Road, Southam, Warwickshire, CV47 0RA
SCHOLASTIC and associated logos are trademarks and/or registered trademarks of
Scholastic Inc.

The Giggler Treatment
First published in the UK by Scholastic Limited, 2000
Text copyright © Roddy Doyle, 2000
Illustration copyright © Brian Ajhar, 2000

Rover Saves Christmas
First published in the UK by Scholastic Limited, 2001
Text copyright © Roddy Doyle, 2001
Illustration copyright © Brian Ajhar, 2001

The Meanwhile Adventures
First published in the UK by Scholastic Limited, 2004
Text copyright © Roddy Doyle, 2004
Illustration copyright © Brian Ajhar, 2004

This edition published 2014

The rights of Roddy Doyle and Brian Ajhar to be identified as the author and
illustrator of this work have been asserted by them.

Cover illustration © Sara Ogilvie, 2014

ISBN 978 1 407 14482 5

Printed and bound by CPI Group (UK) Ltd, Croydon, CR0 44YY
Papers used by Scholastic Children's Books are made from wood grown in
sustainable forests.

5 7 9 10 8 6

www.scholastic.co.uk/zone

Roddy Doyle

The Giggler Treatment

Illustrated by Brian Ajhar

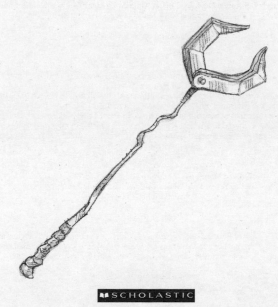

◢SCHOLASTIC

For Kate, Jack and Rory

CHAPTER ONE

Mister Mack was walking to the train station. It was a nice, sunny morning. The birds in the trees were singing their favourite songs. And the breeze that blew was full of breakfast smells – bacon, eggs, frog's legs and cabbage.

"Yum," said Mister Mack to himself.

Mister Mack was feeling happy. Mister Mack was feeling very happy. He had a nice lunch in his lunch box – and a surprise in his flask – and his children's goodbye kisses were still tickling his cheeks. He was going to work, and he liked his job. Actually, Mister Mack loved his job. He was a biscuit tester in a biscuit factory. It was his job to make sure that the biscuits had the right amount of chocolate, if they were supposed to have chocolate. And he measured them to make sure that they were exactly square, if they were supposed to be square, or exactly round, if they were supposed to be round. Best of all, he tasted them. Not all of them. He tasted three in the morning and four in the afternoon, to make sure that they tasted exactly right.

He was looking forward to work because, today, he was going to be testing his favourite biscuits of all time, fig-rolls. The factory made 365 types of biscuits, a different biscuit for every day of the year. Mister Mack liked most of these biscuits, and he loved some of them. But fig-rolls always came top of his list. He loved their shape. He loved their smell. He loved their intelligence. They were such clever biscuits. They were delicious without needing any help from chocolate. And today was a fig-roll-testing day. So Mister Mack was one happy man.

But on his way to the station, just after he'd turned the corner, he saw a seagull sitting on the branch of a tree.

"Do you know what, Mister?" said the seagull. "I hate fish."

"I didn't know seagulls could perch in trees," said Mister Mack.

He kept walking, but he looked back to have another look at the seagull.

And this was a pity, because he didn't see the dog poo right in front of him, on the footpath.

Poor Mister Mack.

His shoe was heading straight for that poo.

CHAPTER TWO

So what?

So what?

Yes. So what? People stand on dog poo all the time. Even dogs stand on dog poo now and again.

But it was huge. It was a big pile of wet, fresh dog poo. It was probably the biggest pile of poo in the world.

Big dog, big poo. So what? I'm bored.

I'm going to skip a few pages and see if there's any more about biscuits.

Wait. Wait! The story isn't about biscuits. And it isn't about the poo. The story is about the people who put the poo on the path so that Mister Mack would stand on it.

The people who put it there? It was dog poo, so it came out of a dog. Right?

Right.

So a dog stopped on the path outside the train station. He stayed there for a little while and left the poo before he ran away. Right?

Wrong. It was dog poo, but it wasn't a dog that put it there. And this story is about the little people who did put it there, just ten seconds before Mister Mack turned the corner.

CHAPTER THREE

Four steps, three steps, two steps.

Mister Mack had seen enough of the seagull. He was going to turn around – in plenty of time to see the poo – but the seagull spoke again.

"Fish," said the seagull. "Don't talk to me about fish."

Four steps, three steps, two steps, one.

Mister Mack's left foot was right over the dog stuff. The bottom of his shoe was exactly sixteen and a half inches from the peak of the poo.

And Mister Mack thought he heard giggles.

And he was right. He had heard giggles. Like these:

"Giggle giggle giggle."

The poo was in the middle of the path. The path was beside a garden wall. And the Gigglers were on the other side of the wall, hidden behind it.

There were three of them. They were all standing on the crossbar of a rusty old bike that had been leaning against the wall for more than twenty years. The bike was so old, it had almost become part of the wall.

The Gigglers had watched Mister Mack as he got nearer to the poo. They had counted the steps.

"How many?"

"Four."

"How many now?"

"Three."

"How many now?"

"Two."

They heard the seagull talking to Mister Mack. And they ducked behind the wall as Mister Mack walked right up to the poo.

"How many now?"

"One."

They waited.

A CHAPTER THAT ISN'T REALLY A CHAPTER BECAUSE NOTHING REALLY HAPPENS IN IT BUT WE'LL CALL IT
CHAPTER FOUR

Nothing happens in this chapter. But some of the questions that are probably hopping about in your heads get answered. Like this one:

Why?

Why what?

Why did the Gigglers put the poo on the path?

Good question. They did it because of

something Mister Mack had done the night before he was walking to the train station. But I'll tell you all about it later because these chapters where nothing happens get boring very quickly.

Now, back to the story.

CHAPTER FIVE
WHICH SHOULD PROBABLY BE CALLED
CHAPTER FOUR
BUT LET'S JUST CALL IT
CHAPTER FIVE

Back at the train station, the Gigglers waited.

They waited for the wallop – Mister Mack hitting the poo.

They waited for the squelch – Mister Mack stepping down on the poo.

They waited for the gasp – Mister Mack seeing the poo for the first time.

They waited for the groan – Mister Mack seeing that most of the poo was now on his shoe.

His shoe was now very, very close to the you-know-what.

"How close?" said the smallest Giggler.

"Fourteen and three-quarter inches," said the biggest Giggler.

"That's very close," said the middle-sized one.

And she shoved her fist into her mouth to trap her giggles.

And they waited.

CHAPTER SIX
WHICH SHOULD PROBABLY BE CALLED
CHAPTER FIVE
IS ANOTHER OF THESE CHAPTERS WHERE NOTHING MUCH HAPPENS EXCEPT FOR ONE VERY EXCITING THING AT THE END

More questions. Like this one:

Who are the Gigglers?

Good question. The Gigglers look after children. And they do it very well. But they do it so quietly that hardly anybody has ever seen them.

How do they look after the children?

Good question. They follow them everywhere. To school, to the shops, to the park, and back home again, upstairs, into the toilet, all over the place. Everywhere the children go, the Gigglers are always near, always looking after them.

What do they look like?

Good question. Only a few people have ever seen the Gigglers and they never tell anyone else about them. So it's hard to tell what the Gigglers look like. They are baby-sized and furry. Their fur changes colour as they move.

Like a chameleon?

Yes, like a chameleon. If they are near a white wall they become white. If they are in a tree they become green and brown. If they are near a car – well, it depends on the colour of the car but they're not very good at being purple, so they try not to go too near to purple cars.

Why do they follow the children?

Another good question. They follow the children to make sure that adults are being fair to them. Parents, teachers, aunties, shopkeepers. All adults. If they are mean to the children, they get the Giggler Treatment. If they send a child to bed without their supper, or if they frighten a child, they get the Giggler Treatment. If they are dishonest to a child, if, say, they give a child fish and say it's chicken, or if they ever fart and then blame the child for it, they get the Giggler Treatment. If they are ever rude to a child or make them wear clothes that they hate, they get the Giggler Treatment.

What is the Giggler Treatment?

Poo on the shoe.

What happens then?

The adults keep getting the Treatment, every day, sometimes twice or three times a day, until they stop being mean to the child.

Have the Gigglers always done this?

Yes, since the beginning of time. The Gigglers have always been there. Since the first dog did its first poo. Since the first caveman grunted at his first cavechild. He stomped out of the cave, straight on to a huge lump of prehistoric poo.

The Roman emperor, Nero, hated children. He ordered his guards to catch all children and feed them to the lions. Then he stood on a dollop of lion poo. (There were more lions than dogs in ancient Rome.) Many years later, a saint called Patrick was busy driving all the snakes out of Ireland. A little boy called Elvis Óg O'Leary, who loved snakes, asked Patrick to stop, but Patrick pushed him out of his way – and walked straight on to a little hill of hot poo that, only seconds before, had been inside an Irish wolfhound called Bran. Saint Patrick got rid of the snakes but he never got rid of the smell.

Two minutes after the *Titanic* hit the iceberg a woman on deck shouted, "Quick, quick! The children will drown!"

"Good," said a man. "There'll be more room in the lifeboats."

And he stepped on to a hill of the slimiest green dog poo and slid off the deck, straight into the sea. "Oh Mammy!"

he roared. "I forgot me water wings!"

So, you see, the Gigglers have been doing this work for thousands of years. All this time they've been giving the Treatment to men and women who are mean to children.

How was Mister Mack mean to his children?

Good question, and the answer is coming up soon. But now we'll go on to the next chapter.

What about the very exciting thing at the end of this chapter?

Oh, yes. I nearly forgot. While I was telling you all about the Gigglers, a woman who was walking in a park in Bombay nearly stood on a snail.

That wasn't exciting.

Well, the snail thought it was.

CHAPTER SEVEN
WHICH SHOULD PROBABLY BE CALLED
CHAPTER FIVE
. . . I THINK . . .
BUT LET'S JUST CALL IT . . .
I DON'T KNOW WHAT
CHAPTER IT'S SUPPOSED TO BE

The Gigglers waited. The shoe was now exactly, exactly, exactly twelve inches and a little bit from the you-know-poo.

"Any second now," whispered the biggest Giggler.

They waited for the thop thop thop – Mister Mack hopping on one foot and trying not to fall over.

They waited for the little thump – Mister Mack leaning against the wall, only three inches of brick and cement away from the Gigglers' noses.

The biggest Giggler looked over the wall, and ducked back down again. "Ten inches," she said.

"Cod?" said the seagull. "Yeuk."

The middle-sized Giggler crammed her other hand and one of her feet into her mouth, to stop the giggles from escaping. She fell off the bike but she made no noise because she landed on soft, long grass.

"Get off," said the grass.

No, it didn't. I'm only messing. But the time has come to explain why the Gigglers were doing this to Mister Mack.

CHAPTER EIGHT
WHICH SHOULD PROBABLY BE CALLED
CHAPTER . . .
HANG ON.
ONE, TWO, THREE, FOUR . . .
OH, STOP MESSING AND
GET ON WITH THE STORY

The day before Mister Mack's foot headed straight for the poo, just before it got too dark to play outside, the Mack brothers, Jimmy and Robbie, broke the kitchen window.

They were playing football with a burst ball when it happened. Robbie Mack gave the ball a whack with his big toe. It bounced off Jimmy Mack's head, flew at the window, and cracked the glass.

"Ouch!" said Robbie. "Me toe!"

"Ouch!" said Jimmy. "Me head!"

"Wah!" said Mister Mack. "Me window!"

He was upstairs when he heard the noise. He was in the bathroom, putting a plaster on his finger. He'd cut his finger putting new glass into the kitchen window, just five minutes before the ball cracked it.

He ran downstairs into the kitchen and saw the broken window. So he kept running, out to the garden. "Who did that?" he shouted.

"Not us," said Robbie. "The ball did it."

"I only just fixed it," said Mister Mack. "It's not fair."

Mister Mack had had a very hard day.

"That's seven times I've had to fix that

window," he said, "in seven days!"

He looked at Robbie and Jimmy.

"Boys, boys, boys," he said. "How many times am I going to have to fix it?"

"Eight," said Robbie.

Robbie wasn't being smart or cheeky when he said that. He was giving Mister Mack the correct answer. The window had been broken seven times, and now he was going to have to fix it once more. Seven and one made eight. So Robbie was right. But poor Mister Mack had had a very hard day. He had spent all day testing cream crackers, and they were very boring biscuits. In fact, Mister Mack didn't think that they were really biscuits at all. They were always perfectly, boringly square and they tasted like nothing except what they were, boring old cream crackers. And poor Mister Mack had been measuring and eating them all day. He was stuffed to the tonsils with cream crackers. He knew he'd dream about cream crackers tonight.

He always had the same cream cracker dream after a day of measuring and eating cream crackers. It wasn't a dream about killer ninja cream crackers or beautiful, brown-eyed cream crackers or anything interesting like that. No chance. In this dream, Mister Mack was always surrounded by talking cream crackers, hundreds of them, all saying the most boring things ever.

"Babies are smaller than adults. Isn't that interesting?"

"Toilet paper is usually white but not always. Isn't that interesting?"

"A car has four wheels but a bike has only two. Isn't that interesting?"

All night the talking cream crackers would be yapping at him. (That was another reason why Mister Mack loved fig-rolls. They never talked when he went to sleep.) He wasn't looking forward to bedtime, even though he was very tired. He could already hear the cream crackers mumbling away in his brain.

"Some pyjamas have stripes and some don't have any stripes at all. Isn't that interesting?"

But that wasn't the worst part of the day. Something strange had happened to Mister Mack at lunchtime. A vulture had swooped down from a tree and robbed his sandwiches.

And, before he'd had time to get over the shock, the vulture came back and robbed his flask. Then he'd had to fix the broken kitchen window for the seventh time in seven days, and he'd cut his finger doing it. He was hungry and tired and his finger was sore and the cream crackers were already yapping at him.

"If you put your feet in water, they get wet. Isn't that interesting?"

The vulture had stuck his tongue out at him as he flew away with the flask. The flask had been full of chicken soup, Mister Mack's all-time favourite. And now, he thought, his children were being cheeky. Mister Mack had had enough.

"Go up to your room," he told Robbie and Jimmy.

"But I'm hungry," said Jimmy.

"I don't care," said Mister Mack. "Go up to your room."

And that was why, the next morning, the poo was waiting for Mister Mack. What Mister Mack didn't know – and what nobody else knew – was that the Gigglers were listening to him. They were in the cupboard under the stairs. They looked at one another and nodded.

"The Treatment?" said the smallest, very quietly.

"The Treatment," said the biggest.

"Poo?" said the smallest.

"Poo," said the biggest.

CHAPTER SOMETHING

Back at the station, the biggest Giggler ducked back down.

"How much now?"

"Eight inches."

And the middle-sized Giggler fell off the bike again.

ANOTHER CHAPTER

Mister Mack went back into the kitchen. The boys' mother, Billie Jean Fleetwood-Mack, was there with the baby, Kayla. Kayla was eating a sugar-free biscuit.

"A-bah," she said.

"No," said Billie Jean. "You can't have one with sugar in it. They're bad for your teeth."

"A-bah," said Kayla.

"I know you don't have any teeth," said

Billie Jean. "But you will soon."

"A-bah."

"Yes, I know your father eats biscuits. It's his job. It's dangerous work," said Billie Jean, proudly. "But somebody has to do it."

She now spoke to Mister Mack. "The boys can't go to bed without their supper," she said.

"I know," said Mister Mack. "I'll call them down in a minute."

"They didn't do it on purpose," said Billie Jean.

"I know," said Mister Mack.

"A-bah," said Kayla.

"I know," said Mister Mack.

"A-bah" was the only word that Kayla could say so far, but because all the Macks loved her so much, they always understood exactly what she meant.

Mister Mack stroked Kayla's cheek.

"It's just, it's been a hard day. You should have seen that vulture."

"A-bah?" said Kayla.

"Even bigger," said Mister Mack.

Then he went into the hall and called up the stairs. "Boys! Come down for your supper!"

"What is it?" Robbie shouted.

"Whatever you want," said Mister Mack. But the Gigglers didn't hear him this time. It was too late. They had gone. They were off looking for the good bit of poo for Mister Mack's shoe.

THE CHAPTER
AFTER THE LAST ONE

They waited for the swipe swipe swipe – Mister Mack rubbing the shoe on some grass.

And the chuff chuff chuff – the train leaving, ha ha.

And the bang bang ouch – Mister Mack banging his head off the wall.

Eight inches.

Seven.

Six.

Five.

They waited for the first big thump – Mister Mack's foot bellyflopping into the you-know-poo.

"Fish fingers?" said the seagull. "Yuk!" The middle-sized Giggler shoved her other foot into her mouth.

Why was it taking so long for Mister Mack's foot to hit the poo?

Good question. Mister Mack was wearing brand-new trousers and they were very stiff. They were so stiff, he could hardly bend and straighten his legs. Now we'll find out where the Gigglers got the you-poo-what.

THE CHAPTER
BEFORE THE NEXT ONE

Dogs don't like going to the toilet on the street. But their owners make them do it.

"Come on, Rover. Let's go for a walk," says Rover's owner as he drags Rover to the front door.

"Let's go for a poo, more like," says Rover to himself. "You're not fooling me."

Poor Rover has to stand out on the street, usually late at night, in the rain and snow, thunder and lightning, in the glare of passing car lights, and go to the toilet while his owner stares straight at him.

"Good boy, Rover. Hurry up," says the owner.

"Leave me alone," says Rover to himself. "My bum is cold."

But Rover does his poo because he knows that he won't get back into the house if he doesn't.

And then the Gigglers come along.

The night that Mister Mack sent the boys up to their bedroom, Rover had done a whopper.

"Wow!" said the Gigglers, rubbing their hands and giggling. "Good old Rover. He never lets us down."

There were four Gigglers there that night. The biggest, the middle-sized, the smallest and the one that was even smaller than the smallest. This was the first time that the even smaller than the smallest Giggler had been out on a poo-finding mission, so she was very excited.

"Are we ready?" said the biggest one.

"Ready."

"Rubber gloves?"

"Rubber gloves."

"Plastic bag?"

"Plastic bag."

"Poo claw?"

"Poo claw."

The smallest Giggler lifted the poo off the path with the poo claw. This was a plastic claw like a crab's that opened and closed when she pushed a lever on its handle.

The middle-sized Giggler held the plastic bag open for the poo.

"Drop the poo," said the biggest Giggler.

"Dropping the poo," said the smallest Giggler.

And she let the poo drop into the plastic bag.

"Catching the poo," said the middle-sized Giggler.

And she closed the bag.

"Well done," said the biggest Giggler. "Twenty pence?"

"Twenty pence," said the even smaller than the smallest Giggler.

This was her big moment.

She took the money from the pouch that covered her green tummy. Her tummy was green because Rover had left the poo right beside a green car.

She held it up in the air. "Twenty pence!"

"Good," said the biggest one. "Let's go."

The money was for Rover. The Gigglers always paid for their poo.

"Rover! Rover!"

The smallest Giggler held the letter box open as the biggest one whisper-shouted into the hall of Rover's house.

Rover was upstairs sitting on the toilet. He always did this when his owner had gone to bed. His owner could never understand how the dog hair got on to the toilet seat or how the paw prints got on to the toilet paper. All dogs do this and they never, ever get caught.

"What now?" said Rover. "Can a dog have no peace?"

He wiped his bum and flushed the toilet. He washed his paws and dried them and went down to the hall. (Rover,

by the way, was the great, great, great –
keep on saying "great" for twenty minutes
– grandson of Bran, the Irish wolfhound.)

Rover saw a Giggler hand sticking
through the letter box holding a twenty-
pence piece. The door was red; the hand
was red.

He took the coin.

"Thanks, Rover," said the even smaller
than the smallest Giggler. "That was a
classic."

"Ure relcon," said Rover, because it's hard to say, "You're welcome" when you are holding a twenty-pence piece between your teeth.

Rover went into the kitchen. He found the big bone his owner had given him earlier that day. (Rover's owner, by the way, was the great, great – keep on saying "great" for two hours and thirty-seven minutes – grandson of the first caveman.) The bone was on the mat. Rover held the bone between his paws and pushed the twenty-pence piece into the hollow part where the marrow used to be.

Rover's owner loved him. He loved the way he shook himself when he was wet. He loved the way he pulled the letters through the letter box when the postman was delivering them, and he didn't mind a bit when Rover made the letters soggy. He was such a clever dog. He could beg. He could fetch sticks. What his owner didn't know – and what nobody else knew

– was that Rover was a millionaire. Rover had buried over a million pounds, all in twenty-pence pieces and all inside hollow bones, in his owner's back garden. All of that money had been given to him by the Gigglers.

"Oh, look at Rover burying the bone. Isn't he clever?"

"Ha ha ha," said Rover to himself. "You'll never know how clever."

Rover hated bones.

THIS CHAPTER
IS NAMED AFTER MY MOTHER
BECAUSE SHE SAID I COULD
STAY UP LATE IF I NAMED IT
AFTER HER
CHAPTER
MAMMY DOYLE

The biggest Giggler looked over the wall.
"Five inches," she said.

"Mackerel?" said the seagull. "Yeuk!"

THIS CHAPTER
IS NAMED AFTER
MY FRIDGE
BECAUSE IT KEEPS
ALL MY FOOD FRESH
CHAPTER FRIDGE

At the exact same time that Mister Mack was heading for the poo, Jimmy Mack fell off a stool in the kitchen as he leaned over to fill his mouth with porridge. The porridge bowl flipped over and landed on Robbie's head.

"Ouch," said Jimmy. "Me bum!"

"Ouch!" said Robbie. "Me head!"

Billie Jean came into the kitchen. She was wearing big boots and snow goggles. She had a long rope tied around her waist. She was carrying Kayla on her back and she was sweating.

Billie Jean was a mountain climber. She practised her climbing every day by running up the stairs with Kayla on her back. She did this for three hours every morning and rested only once, for five minutes, in a tent she'd pitched in the hall.

Billie Jean wanted to climb the highest mountain in every country in the world. She'd already climbed a lot of them, in Argentina, Kenya, Australia and lots of other countries.

The first mountain she'd ever climbed was in Holland. Holland is a very flat country, and its highest mountain is only ten feet high. It's so small, nobody had ever given it a name. But when Billie Jean got to the top she named it Mister Mack Mountain, after her all-time favourite husband. (Billie Jean, by the way, was the great, great – keep saying "great" for twenty minutes – granddaughter of Elvis Óg O'Leary, the little boy who tried to keep the snakes in Ireland.)

The next mountain Billie Jean was going to climb was Blue Mountain Peak in Jamaica. She was leaving the biggest one, Mount Everest in Nepal, until last. She wanted to wait until Kayla was older and then they would climb it together. Kayla was looking forward to it. All that running up the stairs on her mammy's back had given her a love of heights and adventure.

"What happened?" said Billie Jean when she saw Jimmy on the floor.

"I broke me bum," said Jimmy.

She laughed. "There's half an hour to go

before school," she said. "Why don't you go on out and play."

Jimmy forgot about his sore bum and ran out the back door.

"Bring Kayla with you," said Billie Jean.

"OK," said Robbie as he rubbed some of the porridge off his hair with a tea towel. "Come on, Kayla."

He put Kayla on to his shoulders. "Hang on to my hair," he said.

"A-bah?" said Kayla.

"It's OK," Robbie told her. "It's only porridge."

They ran around to the front of the house and played with the burst ball.

Kayla sat on top of the wall and pretended she was on top of Mount Everest. She was a good balancer, but just to be safe, the boys stuck wet chewing gum to the wall and put her down on top of it. She was very happy up there, watching the leaves tickling one another in the tree above her and her mad brothers playing below her.

Robbie was the goalkeeper, and Jimmy kicked the ball to him. Robbie's hands missed the ball, but he caught it with his face. It bounced off his nose, hit Jimmy's elbow, and bounced again under an old oil drum.

"Ouch!" said Jimmy. "Me elbow!"

"Ouch!" said Robbie. "Me doze!"

The drum was upside down and heavy, too heavy for the boys to lift. It had been there for years, since long before the Macks had lived there. Mister Mack said that it had fallen out of the sky and that the Wicked Witch of the East was under it, but the Mack brothers weren't sure about that. Anyway, the ball was under it now.

"Now what will we do?" said Robbie.

"A-bah," said Kayla.

"Good idea, Kayla," said Robbie.

The boys ran off and got one of Billie Jean's mountain-climbing ropes from the shed. They came back and tied one end of the rope around the oil drum. Then they threw the other end up over a branch of the tree.

"Now what?" said Jimmy.

"A-bah."

"Brilliant idea."

They lifted Kayla until she held the other end of the rope. She dangled happily, but she wasn't heavy enough to budge the bin.

"A-bah," she said.

"Mega-brilliant idea."

The boys gathered some stones and put them into Kayla's nappy. She became heavier and heavier. As she dropped slowly, slowly to the ground, the bin was slowly, slowly lifted. There was soon a space big enough for Jimmy, and he crawled under the drum.

"Can you see the ball?" Robbie shouted.

"No!" Jimmy shouted back.

"Well, what can you see?"

"A monster!"

CHAPTER
TWO MILLION
AND SEVEN

"I'm not a monster," the monster said to Jimmy.

"What are you then?" said Jimmy.

"A Giggler," said the even smaller than the smallest Giggler.

Robbie grabbed Jimmy's legs and pulled him out from under the drum. And the Giggler followed Jimmy.

"Hello," she said, and she rubbed her hands and giggled. "Any second now."

"Any second now what?" said Robbie.

"Your dad's shoe will hit the poo."

"A-bah?" said Kayla.

"Rover's," said the Giggler.

And she came out from under the drum and stood up.

Hang on a minute.

How come they could see her? Aren't Gigglers supposed to be like chameleons? Aren't they able to change colour?

Good questions. Yes, they are able to change colour, but a few days before they met the even smaller than the smallest Giggler, the boys had painted the oil drum purple, and Gigglers, remember, aren't very good at being purple. So they could see her clearly. She was bright blue against the purple drum.

"A-bah?" said Kayla.

"We put it there," said the Giggler, "so your dad would walk on it."

"Why?" said Robbie.

"Because he sent you up to your room last night," said the Giggler.

"But he only sent us up for a minute," said Robbie.

"Oh-oh," said the even smaller than the smallest Giggler.

"A-bah," said Kayla.

And the Giggler agreed with her. "Yes," she said. "It is a terrible waste of poo."

Next door, Rover was burying his bone in the flower bed.

"Well, you're not getting your money back," he said to himself as he kicked muck on top of the bone.

"And it's not fair either," said Jimmy. "We'll have to warn him."

"A-bah," said Kayla.

"Good idea," said Jimmy, and he ran to get their mother, who was the fastest runner in the house.

"I've an idea," said the Giggler. "Rover!"

"Oh-oh," said Rover, in the garden beside them.

He tried to be more dog-like. He chased a fly, he scratched himself, he went woof-woof and snarled at a pair of knickers hanging on the washing line.

"Rover!"

He heard the Giggler's voice.

"Rover!"

It was a special call, like a dog whistle. Only dogs could hear a Giggler's call. And all dogs had to obey when the Giggler's called, even clever, sparky dogs like

54

Rover. But Rover wasn't going to give up. "Rover!"

"I can't hear you!" he shouted. "I've got a cold."

"Rover!" said the Giggler. "Jump over the wall."

"I've got a bad back."

"I'll pay you fifty pence," said the Giggler.

And Rover jumped the wall without a bother and landed right in front of the Giggler. "I take all the major credit cards," he said.

Then he saw Kayla and Robbie looking at him.

"So. I can talk," he said. "Have you got anything to say about that?"

"No," said Robbie.

"No?" said Rover. "You're not surprised? I'm a dog and I can talk."

"We know you can talk," said Robbie. "We've heard you. You're always muttering and giving out when you're digging in your garden."

"Am I?" said Rover.

"Yeah," said Robbie.

"How long have you known?" said Rover.

"A-bah," said Kayla.

"That long?" said Rover. "I'd better be more careful. The adults might hear me."

"Don't worry," said Robbie. "The adults don't listen. They just think you're barking."

He turned back to the Giggler. "So, what's the story, Gig?"

"Mister Mack's foot is heading for your poo. We have to stop him."

"My poo!" said Rover. "If he lands in it, he'll never escape. It's the best poo in the business. It's super-poo."

He ran to the wall. "Hop on, kid."

And Kayla jumped down, on to his back.

"Hang on to my ears," said Rover, and

he ran out the gate, and headed for the train station.

The Giggler jumped on to Robbie's back.

"Follow that baby," she said.

And Robbie ran.

Billie Jean ran out of the house with Jimmy on her back.

"Follow that Giggler," said Jimmy.

And Billie Jean kept running.

CHAPTER SIXTEEN
(THIS CHAPTER, BY THE WAY, IS THE GREAT, GREAT, GREAT, GREAT, GREAT, GREAT, GREAT, GREAT, GREAT, GREAT, GREAT, GREAT, GREAT, GREAT GRANDSON OF CHAPTER ONE)

Back at the station, Mister Mack finally turned away from the seagull.

"Goldfish?" said the seagull. "Yeuk."

But Mister Mack wasn't interested any more. He turned his head.

In time to see the poo?

No. His foot was right over the poo now AND the poo was shaped exactly like a shoe. So Mister Mack couldn't see it.

Shoe-shaped poo. It looked exactly like the shoe's shadow. It was a trick Rover had practised over the years, and a lot of dedication and dog food had gone into getting it right.

DON'T TRY IT AT HOME, KIDS, UNLESS THERE'S AN ADULT WITH YOU.

"How much now?" said the middle-sized Giggler.

"Three inches."

"My goodness," said Mister Mack. "These are the all-time stiffest trousers I've ever worn."

And he thought he heard a dog barking.

THIS CHAPTER IS NAMED AFTER
ELVIS PRESLEY
BECAUSE HE LIVES UNDER THE
SHED IN OUR BACK GARDEN

Mister Mack did hear a dog.

But it wasn't Rover.

It was just a dog.

Rover wasn't really a barking kind of dog. Actions speak louder than woofs, was Rover's motto. And, right now, Rover was probably the most active dog in the world.

He ran like the wind's big brother with Kayla, his baby jockey, on his back. He galloped so fast, his paws hardly touched the ground.

"This is cool," said his left paw, the front one.

"Good old Rover," said the right paw. "He's a flyer."

"A-bah?" said Kayla.

"Yep," said Rover. "I'm the only dog in the world with talking paws. Hang on tight."

And he galloped past the shops – the bread shop, the sweet shop, the twirly coloured pasta-that's-very-nice-with-cheese shop.

Rover was fast. And so was Robbie. Even with the Giggler on his back, he was faster than Rover, and he was catching up.

Past the bread shop, the sweetshop.

And Billie Jean was faster still. Even with Jimmy on her back and heavy mountain boots on her feet, she was zooming down the street and catching up with Robbie.

Past the twirly coloured pasta-that's-very-nice-with-cheese shop.

Rover, Robbie and Billie Jean – they were the fastest things on eight feet.

But would they be quick enough?

A VERY SHORT
CHAPTER
TO LET YOU KNOW HOW MANY INCHES
MISTER MACK'S FOOT WAS
AWAY FROM THE POO

Two.

THERE IS MORE THAN ONE SIDE TO EVERY STORY, AND THIS STORY HAS LOTS OF SIDES:

THE CREAM CRACKERS GIVE THEIR SIDE OF THE STORY

We weren't there. We saw nothing. Isn't that interesting?

A REAL CHAPTER

Rover ran.

The clothes shop, the toy shop, the colouring pencil shop.

As he ran past the pet shop he looked at the doggies in the window. "So long, suckers!" he shouted.

The shoe shop, the sock shop, the grandfather clock shop.

Robbie and Billie Jean caught up with him.

"Do you know any good shortcuts, Rover?" said Robbie.

"Woof," said Rover.

He wasn't going to talk in front of an adult, he didn't care how nice she was.

ROVER
GIVES HIS SIDE
OF THE STORY

Shhhhh.

I have to be very quiet. If my owner wakes up and catches me typing on his computer, I'll have a lot of explaining to do. I can just hear him:

"How did Rover plug it in?"

"Just what exactly was Rover doing in here?"

"How did Rover know how to spell his name?"

He nearly caught me last week. I was sending an e-mail to my girlfriend in Galway. Her family moved there a few months ago, and I've a feeling I miss her more than she misses me. Anyway, there I am, writing her a love poem, trying to think of a good word to rhyme with "Lassie" – that's her name, by the way – when I hear the owner turning on the bedside light. I was out of here and downstairs on my mat before his feet hit the floor. Then he must have noticed that the computer was on. And do you know what he said?

"Who put the paw marks on the mouse?"

Can you believe that? Who lives here, for Dog's sake? The owner, his wife, four big kids, and one dog. The owner, his wife, and the four big kids have hands and feet, and the one dog has paws.

"Who put the paw marks on the mouse?" the man asks.

Anyway, I still have to be careful, even if my owner isn't exactly a master detective.

There's only one thing I want to say. If I had known that the Gigglers were going to use my poo on the Mack guy's shoe I would never have sold it to them. I swear to Dog, I would never have done it. I have to make a living and I like what the Gigglers do – I like their style. But I've seen the Mack guy playing with his kids. He's a good father, a loving husband, all that corny stuff. He brings biscuits home from work and he often throws a few over the wall to good old Rover. OK, they're not exactly fresh, but it's the thought that counts.

I like the guy. And I'll say this: if Rover likes a guy, he doesn't go around pooing on his shoe.

Anyway, that's all I wanted to say. I'd better get out of here. The owner is mumbling in his sleep. That means he's going to get up for a pee or a sandwich.

I'm out of here. Double click.

HOW MANY
INCHES NOW?

One.

Just one inch. The sole of Mister Mack's shoe was an inch – less than an inch – from the tip of the poo.

Where were Rover and Kayla? Where were Robbie and the even smaller than the smallest Giggler? Where were Billie Jean and Jimmy?

Two-thirds of an inch.

Half an inch.

Less than half an inch.

Where were they?

WELL,
WHERE WERE THEY?

Rover knew a shortcut. Rover knew every shortcut in town. Rover knew every shortcut in the world.

Rover ran, and the others followed him. He ran down a lane beside the cake shop. At the end of the lane, a wall – Rover jumped – and at the other side, a small river –

"Hang on, kid."

Rover jumped.

His back paws touched the water, his

nails scratched the riverbank, mud and stones fell back into the river. But Rover had made it across.

"A-bah," said Kayla.

"Thanks, toots," said Rover.

He kept running.

Robbie jumped but he was going to fall into the river – he hadn't jumped far enough. He held his nose and got ready for the splash, when Billie Jean, in mid-air, grabbed the back of Robbie's shirt and continued on her jump across the river.

They all landed in a big heap on the other bank.

"Isn't this great fun?" said Billie Jean.

"Don't forget the poo, Mum," said Jimmy.

"Oh, yes," said Billie Jean.

And they were off again, after Rover and Kayla.

HOW FAR NOW?

Less than less than half an inch.

The Gigglers behind the wall got their ears ready. Oh, they loved that sweet sound. The glorious squelch of an adult foot sinking into the best poo that money could buy. It was music to their furry ears.

Mister Mack could hear the train coming.

KAYLA
GIVES HER SIDE
OF THE STORY

A-bah.
  A-bah, a-bah.
  A-bah, a-bah, a-bah.
  A-bah.
  A-bah, a-bah, a-bah, a-bah, a-bah.
  A-bah.
  A-bah, a-bah, a-bah –
  A-bah.

JIMMY AND ROBBIE
GIVE THEIR SIDE
OF THE STORY

JIMMY: We think it's a brilliant idea.

ROBBIE: Yes, we do.

JIMMY: Giving adults the Giggler Treatment.

ROBBIE: Making them walk on poo.

JIMMY: It's fair and it's funny.

ROBBIE: It's very funny.

JIMMY: But if we'd known that the

Gigglers were going to give our daddy the Treatment –

ROBBIE: If we'd known –

JIMMY: I think we would have tried to stop them sooner.

ROBBIE: We probably would have.

JIMMY: Even though it's funny.

ROBBIE: Even though it's brilliant.

JIMMY: It's the funniest thing ever.

ROBBIE: Funnier even than doing rudies in the bath.

ROBBIE: We probably would have warned him.

JIMMY: Probably.

ROBBIE: Even though the ball broke the window, not us.

JIMMY: And even though he wouldn't let me put one of Kayla's nappies in the toaster to see what would happen.

ROBBIE: And even though he wouldn't let me make a kite out of Granny's knickers, and she wasn't even wearing them.

JIMMY: And even though he wouldn't let me pick my nose, even though there was a brilliant bit of snot up there and I wanted to flick it at Grandad because he was asleep and his mouth was open.

ROBBIE: And even though he wouldn't let me slide off the roof with Kayla on my head.

JIMMY: We would probably have tried to stop the Gigglers sooner.

ROBBIE: Even though it was really funny.

JIMMY: Really, really funny.

WHAT'S KEEPING ROVER?

Rover ran across a field. He ran across a road. He ran across the Sahara Desert.

"A-bah?" said Kayla.

"Yeah, kid," said Rover. "It's the Sahara. Trust me."

Billie Jean caught up with Rover. "Are you sure this is the way?"

"Woof," said Rover.

Robbie caught up with them. "We never went this way to the station before," he said.

"Woof," said Rover.

They climbed over a huge sand dune, and there in front of them, was a huge, wide river.

"Oh my goodness," said Billie Jean. "It's the river Nile."

"Cool," said Jimmy.

"Lift your legs, kid," Rover whispered to Kayla.

And he ran into the water, and swam when it got too deep for his legs. Robbie followed Rover. He was an excellent swimmer, even with the Giggler on his back. And Billie Jean followed Robbie. She couldn't swim but Jimmy could, so she held on to his trousers.

Rover swam across the river. "See that log, kid?" he said.

"A-bah."

"Well, it's a crocodile," said Rover.

It was a crocodile. It was a vegetarian crocodile, the only veggie croc in the river that day.

"Bet you wish I was a carrot," Rover said to the croc as they swam past him.

They swam to the far side and climbed the sandy bank.

"Not far now, kid," said Rover.

NOT FAR!!

Measure a mouse's eyelash. Not down. Across. That was how far Mister Mack's shoe was from the poo.

And his rescuers were in Egypt!

In North Africa!

They'd never make it on time.

WHERE IN THE WORLD IS ROVER?

Rover climbed the steep, sandy bank of the river Nile – and saw, right in front of him, the Eiffel Tower.

"Yes!" said Rover. "Ha, ha. Just as I expected."

He ran.

THE SEAGULL
GIVES HIS SIDE
OF THE STORY

Fish?
 Fish?
 Don't talk to me about fish.
 I hate fish.
 Cod?
 Yeuk.
 Salmon?
 Yeuk.

Jellyfish?

Yeuk.

Herring, haddock, halibut?

Yeuk, yeuk, yeuk.

Fish fingers?

Yeuk.

Fish toes? Fish necks, elbows, knees, eyes, fish teeth, fish hair, fish glasses?

Yeuk, yeuk, yeuk for a million years.

Fish?

If I had my way I'd round them all up and throw them into the sea.

WHERE IN
THE WORLD
IS ROVER?
(II)

Rover ran to the Eiffel Tower, through the tourists and ice-cream sellers.

A man with a flowery shirt and a video camera stood in his way.

"What's the matter, pal?" said Rover as he ran between the man's legs. "Did you never see a baby on a dog's back before?" The man's mouth dropped open.

"Did that dog just talk?" he asked his wife, whose mouth had also dropped open.

"I . . . think . . . so?" she said.

"How come he didn't speak French?" said the man.

"Maybe he's on his holiday, too," said the woman.

"Ah," said the man. "That explains it."

Under the Eiffel Tower, beside one of the giant metal legs that lifted the tower to the sky, Rover found what he was looking for. It was a rabbit hole, hidden under a bush, and Rover dived into it.

He ran through the dark of the tunnel. They could hear the others behind them. They ran and they ran.

Then they saw it – a tiny dot of light in front of them.

They ran and they ran, and the dot got bigger and bigger, but it was still very small, still far away. They ran and they ran and now the dot was getting bigger and much brighter.

Rover was getting tired. He was panting and thirsty.

He took one last breath, and ran – and jumped into the bright, bright light – and landed in the garden, right behind the Gigglers on the bike.

"Mind the poo!" he shouted.

Kayla flew off Rover's back, over the bike and the Gigglers' heads, right over the wall and landed in her father's arms.

"A-bah!"

Mister Mack looked down.

Too late.

His foot was in the poo. The left leg of his brand-new trousers was up to its knee in Rover's –

"Stop right there."

Yes, Rover?

"Are you saying that I was too late?"

Yes, Rover.

"Are you seriously saying that I was too late? After all that? The Mack guy's foot ends up in the stink?"

Yes, Rover. You see, it's funnier if Mister Mack's shoe –

"Forget funnier, pal. And listen. See these teeth?"

Yes, Rover.

"Now they're funny. See your ankle?"

Yes, Rover.

"My teeth get to know your ankle. Now that's what I call funny. Ha, ha, ha. Do you understand me, pal?"

Yes, Rover.

"Well, then. Was Rover too late?"

No, Rover.

"Good. We'll start again."

Yes, Rover.

ROVER
SAVES THE DAY

Rover was getting tired. He was panting
and thirsty. But brave Rover kept running.
He took one last breath – and brave,
handsome Rover jumped into the bright,
bright light – and landed in the garden,
right behind the Gigglers on the bike.

"Mind the poo!" he shouted.

Kayla flew off Rover's back, over the
bike and the Gigglers' heads, right over
the wall and landed in her father's arms.

"A-bah!"

Mister Mack looked down.

Just in time.

His shoe was right there, right bang on top of the poo. How near? How close? The shoe was kissing the poo.

Mister lifted his foot and walked right over the poo.

And now, Rover jumped over the wall. Followed by Robbie and the even smaller than the smallest Giggler.

Followed by Jimmy and Billie Jean.

Followed by the other three Gigglers, biggest, middle-sized and smallest.

Hang on a minute.

How come they could see the Gigglers?

When they want to be seen, the Gigglers can be seen. They stopped being grey, the colour of the wall, and became bright blue in exactly three seconds.

Billie Jean looked at the poo and at Mister Mack's shoe. "Oh, thank goodness, you're safe," she said.

"Yes," said Mister Mack. "But if it hadn't

been for. . . Hang on," said Mister Mack. "You did say, 'Mind the poo.'"

"A-bah," said Kayla.

"You, Kayla?" said Mister Mack. "Your first words! 'Mind the poo!' This is the happiest day of my life. Say it again, Kayla. Say, 'Mind the poo.'"

"A-bah," said Kayla.

"She said it again!" said Mister Mack.

He kissed her forehead. He held her over his head. He laughed.

"For a minute there I thought it was the dog that said it."

"Woof," said Rover.

"Dogs can't talk, Dad," said Jimmy.

"Woof," said Rover.

"Who ever heard of a dog talking?" said Robbie.

"Take it easy, pal," Rover whispered. "You're overdoing it."

The biggest Giggler came up to Mister Mack.

"Sorry about the poo," she said.

"What about the poo?" said Mister Mack.

She explained about adults being mean to children, and dog poo, and Rover, and plastic bags and shoes.

"But we made a mistake with you," she said.

"That's OK," said Mister Mack. "Keep up the good work. The vulture doesn't work for you, does he?"

"No," said the smallest Giggler. "But we know him. He doesn't really like being a vulture. He much prefers sandwiches to dead bodies."

"I'll share mine with him," said Mister Mack. "But not today."

Mister Mack had a trick up his sleeve. Well, actually, it wasn't up his sleeve. It was in his flask. He had filled the flask with orange juice, with "bits". And, as everybody knows, vultures don't like "bits". He was looking forward to lunchtime but he said nothing to the Gigglers.

"Would you all like to come back to our house for breakfast?" said Billie Jean.

"We'd love to," said the biggest Giggler. "But there's a woman waiting for the Giggler Treatment. She wouldn't let her kids watch telly because they didn't finish their parsnips."

"Oh, the mean old thing," said Billie Jean.

"She'll be walking to the train station in a few minutes," said the biggest Giggler. "We need some of the fresh stuff. Rover?"

The middle-sized Giggler handed a twenty-pence piece to Rover.

"Put your money back in your pouch, pal," said Rover, very quietly. "This one's on me."

He walked past Kayla.

"It's a dog's life," he whispered. "Bye bye, kid."

And he walked behind a bush, humming a song called "How Much Is That Human in the Window?"

The middle-sized Giggler followed him with a plastic bag. The smallest Giggler followed with her poo claw. And the even smaller than the smallest Giggler followed them and, as they walked away, they became green like the bush, and disappeared.

Then Mister Mack heard the train leaving the station. "Oh no," he said. "I'm going to be late for work. The fig-rolls will be all gone. I'll be tasting cream crackers again. All day."

He could already hear them.

"When grass gets long, you cut it with a lawn mower. Isn't that interesting?"

"If you close your eyes, you can't see. Isn't that interesting?"

But Kayla saved the day again. "A-bah," she said.

"Chocolate-covered cream crackers!" said Mister Mack. "What a brilliant idea! Thanks, Kayla."

"Fish-covered cream crackers?" said the seagull.

He flew off his branch.

"I'm going back to the sea," he said. "Well away from fish."

But Mister Mack didn't hear him. He was running to the train station. He could already taste the new, exciting, chocolate cream crackers. He could already hear them.

"In 1984, a man ate thirteen raw eggs in one second. Isn't that interesting?"

"A man once pulled two train carriages with his teeth. Isn't that interesting?"

Mister Mack was one happy man.

A CHAPTER
THAT ISN'T REALLY
A CHAPTER
BECAUSE THE STORY ENDED
AT THE END OF THE
LAST CHAPTER

All good stories have messages, and this story has loads of them. Here are some of them:

1. If a vulture ever robs your sandwiches, remember, he's only doing it because he doesn't want to eat you. (The vulture, by the way, was the great, great –

keep saying great for two hours and twenty-seven minutes – grandson of the pterodactyl that pooed on the first caveman's head the day after he stepped on the first prehistoric dog poo.)

2. Something else.

3. Your dog might not talk to you, but that doesn't mean that he or she can't talk. Also, not all dogs are millionaires, only the ones that poo a lot.

4. The seagull – make one up yourself.

5. If you have a baby like Kayla Mack in your house, always listen to her advice, especially if it has anything to do with chocolate and cream crackers.

6. And last, if you are an adult and you ever walk on dog poo, ask yourself, "Why are the Gigglers giving me the Giggler Treatment?" But remember, it might not be the Giggler Treatment. It might just be poo.

THE END

"Hey, pal."

Oh, yes. Sorry, Rover. I nearly forgot.

7. If your name is Lassie and you live in Galway, Rover says hi.

THE END

Roddy Doyle

Rover Saves Christmas

Illustrated by Brian Ajhar

■SCHOLASTIC

To Santa

Thanks to Abel Ugba for his advice,
and to Thomas Gromoff, for
the Finnish word for "poo".
R.D.

To Rebecca Lynn
B.A.

CHAPTER ONE

It was Christmas Eve in Dublin and the sun was splitting the rocks. The lizards were wearing flip-flops and the cacti that line the streets of the city were gasping.

"Water!" gasped a cactus.

"Diet water!" gasped his girlfriend beside him.

The River Liffey had dried up and the tyres on all the city's buses had melted. Robbie and Jimmy Mack were frying an egg on a shovel and—

Hang on.

Yes?

Dublin isn't like that at Christmas. Start again.

OK.

It was Christmas Eve in Dublin and it had been snowing for weeks. Snowflakes the size of mice fell from the grey sky and the cacti that line the streets of the city were very cold and confused. Jimmy and Robbie Mack were trying to scrape a frozen egg off a shovel and—

Stop.

Yes?

Dublin isn't like that either. Stop being silly or I won't buy the book.

Sorry.

It was Christmas Eve in Dublin and it was raining. It had been raining for weeks and the cacti that line the streets of the city were sick of it.

"I'm full," said a cactus.

"I'm fat," said his girlfriend beside him.

Robbie and Jimmy Mack threw eggs at each other because there was no snow to make snowballs. One egg skidded on the wet grass and rolled under a wet, dripping bush. It stopped beside a lizard.

The lizard looked at the egg. He didn't want to eat it.

"Why not?" said the egg.

He was too cold to eat it. He was stiff and damp and miserable. He turned bright red, because he hoped that that would make him warm. But it didn't.

"What a lovely colour," said a voice beside him.

It was a lovely voice. It was the loveliest voice the lizard had ever heard. He looked, and saw the loveliest lizard he had ever seen. And he stayed red, because he was blushing.

"You look warm," said the loveliest lizard.

"Oh," said the lizard. "Actually, I'm very cold."

And, gradually, he stopped being red and became a much colder colour, grey.

"Are *you* not cold?" he said.

"No," said the loveliest lizard. "I have the right name."

"What do you mean?"

"Well," said the loveliest lizard. "I change my name whenever the weather changes. When it's very hot I choose a name from a hot country, and I feel fine. And when it's very cold or wet, like now, I choose a name from a colder country. What's *your* name?" she asked.

"Omar."

"Nice name," she said. "But not right for this weather. Try calling yourself 'Hans'. That's a nice cold name."

"OK," said Omar.

He coughed, and spoke. "My name is 'Hans'."

"How does that feel?" said the loveliest lizard.

Hans lowered his tummy down to the cold, wet grass.

"Nice," he said. "Very nice."

He rubbed his tummy on the grass. He began to glow; he was becoming silver. "Very, very nice. What's *your* name?" he asked.

"Heidi," said the loveliest lizard.

"Hi-dee-hi, Heidi," said Hans.

"Hi-dee-ho, Hans," said Heidi.

Hans flicked his long tongue and

caught a fly that was resting on a wall far away, in Morocco.

"Wow," said Heidi.

"Care to share some spicy wings?" said Hans.

Hans chewed and smiled at Heidi. Heidi chewed and smiled at Hans. They were full of fly and falling in love. But this story isn't about Hans and Heidi, although they're in it. And it definitely isn't about the fly. (He was tumbling down into Heidi's tummy, humming a sad song called "Torn Between Two Lizards".) The story is about Robbie and Jimmy and a dog and some other people and what they did on Christmas Eve.

It starts on the next page, Chapter Two. And that means that you just wasted your time reading Chapter One. Sorry.

CHAPTER TWO

Jimmy and Robbie Mack were very excited and very bored. It was Christmas Eve and they wanted the day to end, so they could go to bed and wake up the next morning.

Christmas Day.

The best day in the whole year.

They'd been thinking about nothing else for months.

"What do you want for breakfast?" their mother had asked Jimmy last October.

"Christmas," said Jimmy.

"What is the capital of France?" their teacher, Mister Eejit, had asked on the last day before the holidays.

"Presents," said Robbie.

Robbie and Jimmy had been extra-specially good for the last few weeks. For example, they had helped their Granda to find his false teeth. They were super-glued to the roof of his car. (Jimmy and Robbie had glued the teeth to the roof but it is much more important to know that they had helped poor old Granda to find them. And, by the way, they got the teeth off the roof with a can opener.) They'd spent all their pocket-money on presents for the people they loved — *Banjo-Kazooie* for their mother, a new uniform for Granny's Action Man, a special pair of scissors for their father for cutting the horrible big hairs that grew out of his ears and nose, a T-shirt with BARNEY SMOKES BIG FAT CIGARS on it for their baby sister and a brand new can opener for Granda. (The old one was stuck in the roof of his car.)

They had tied their stockings to the ends of their beds. They had made twenty-seven cheese sandwiches and left them in a huge pile on the mantelpiece for Santa. They had cut the crusts off the sandwiches because Santa never ate the crusts. And they had left one of their mother's cans of Guinness on the mantelpiece beside the sandwiches, and a carrot for Rudolph.

But there were still hours and hours to go before bedtime.

"How long now?" said Jimmy.

"Thirteen hours and thirty-seven minutes," said Robbie.

"I think I'll make another sandwich for Santa."

"I think I'll peel Rudolph's carrot."

The brothers were walking to the back door. They were soaking wet and hungry and excited and bored and their little sister jumped out of an upstairs window of the house next door.

CHAPTER THREE

Kayla Mack floated down under a parachute she'd made from half her best friend's mother's best dress. And Victoria, her best friend, followed her, hanging on to the other half of her mother's best dress.

It used to be a beautiful dress, and now it was two beautiful parachutes.

WARNING!

Don't try this at home, kids. Jumping out of upstairs windows is not a good idea. You could break your arm or your leg or your head or, if the window is shut, you could even break the glass. Also, in real life, dresses don't make good, safe parachutes, and half-dresses are even worse. So, don't jump, kids. Use the stairs. And, while we're at it, if you ever cut your mother's best dress in two, don't make parachutes out of it.

Just throw it in a corner and blame the cat. Leave the scissors beside the cat's mat and blow-dry his or her hair to make it look like he or she has been jumping out of aeroplanes all day. However, before you blame the cat, first make sure that you actually have one.

Now, back to the story.

It used to be a beautiful dress, and now it was two beautiful parachutes.

"Oh, man!" said Jimmy.

"Good on yourself, Kayla!" said Robbie.

They watched Kayla flying over their heads, carried on the wind. Her feet just missed the branches of an apple tree, and she landed in the centre of the garden, bang in the middle of the flower bed.

Robbie and Jimmy ran to congratulate her.

And then they saw the elf.

Because Kayla had landed on him.

"Get off me, please," said the elf.

"Who are you?" said Kayla.

"I'm too busy to answer that question," said the elf.

He looked very unhappy and wet. He was wearing a black leather jacket, with HELL'S ELVES printed on its back.

He got out from under Kayla, and Victoria landed on him.

"Get off me, please," said the elf. "I'm a busy man."

"Who are you?" said Kayla.

"Bum-bum," said Victoria.

"I told you," said the elf. "I'm too busy to answer."

"Who are you?"

"Bum-bum."

The elf took a notebook from the pocket of his jacket.

"Are you two being cheeky?" he said. "You'd better not be."

"Who are you?" said Kayla.

"That does it," said the elf. "You're going into me book. What's your name?"

"Who are you?"

"Bum-bum."

"What's your name?" said the elf.

"Who are you?"

"Bum-bum."

The elf took a pencil out from behind his very big ear. By the way, his other ear was very big too, and there was an earring hanging from it – a very small silver ear.

"Who are you?" said Kayla.

INTERRUPTION

You're probably wondering why Kayla kept saying, "Who are you?"

Well, the answer is easy.

She couldn't say anything else.

CHAPTER THREE

The elf flicked through the notebook. "Who are you?" said Kayla.

RETURN OF THE
INTERRUPTION

Sorry for interrupting again but you need to know a little bit more about Kayla. She was one and a half and a bit. And she had only started talking. "Who are you?" were her first real words. But, because everybody who knew her loved her so much, they always knew exactly what she meant.

Here is what she actually said to the elf:

ELF: Get off me, please.

KAYLA: I'm very sorry.

VICTORIA: Bum-bum.

Oops. I forgot to explain about Victoria.

Victoria was the same age as Kayla, the exact same age. They were born at the exact same moment, in the same hospital, in the same ward, but not on the same bed. And now they lived next-door to each other. "Bum-bum" was or were Victoria's first word or words. But, because everybody who knew her loved her so much, they always knew exactly what *she* meant.

ELF: Get off me, please.

KAYLA: I'm very sorry.

VICTORIA: Ouch, me bum.

ELF: I'm too busy to answer that question.

KAYLA: Are you an elf?

VICTORIA: Are you an elf?

ELF: I told you. I'm too busy to answer.

KAYLA: Do you work for Santa?

VICTORIA: Are you spying on us?

ELF: Are you being cheeky? You'd better not be.

KAYLA: We've been really good.

VICTORIA: We'll stitch the dress back together again.

ELF: That does it. You're going into me book. What's your name?

KAYLA: Kayla.

VICTORIA: Victoria.

ELF: What's your name?

The elf took a pencil out from behind his very big ear. By the way, his other ear was very big too. So was his nose and both of his feet.

"Excuse me," said Jimmy.

"What?" said the elf.

"Stop being so grumpy."

And the elf kind of slumped.

"I'm sorry," he said. "It's just, I'm so busy."

"Who are you?" said Kayla.

"Yes," said the elf. "I do work for Santa."

He jumped, and pointed at Kayla.

"I understood her!"

"That's because you're not grumpy any more," said Robbie.

"Bum-bum," said Victoria.

"Thank you," said the elf.

A huge drop of rain fell from a branch and whacked the elf on the nose.

"Oh yes!" he said, as if he was waking up. "I'm looking for, for, for –"

He opened his notebook and flicked from page to page.

"For, for, for, for, for – oh yes. Rover. I'm looking for something called Rover."

"A dog?" said Jimmy.

The elf looked into the notebook again.

"A cat, a rat, a duck? Ah yes – a dog."

"He lives next door," said Robbie.

"Oh great, then I've found him."

"Why do you want him?" said Jimmy.

"I don't want him," said the elf. "The boss does. You see, Rudolph's gone on strike."

CHAPTER FOUR

WARNING:
WEAR GLOVES AND A HAT
WHEN YOU'RE READING THIS
CHAPTER BECAUSE IT TAKES
PLACE IN LAPLAND, IN THE
NORTH OF FINLAND, AND
IT'S VERY COLD THERE

"Please, Rudolph," said Santa.

"No, man," said Rudolph. "No can do."

They were in the barn behind Santa's house and workshop. Outside, elves on snowmobiles and sledges pulled by husky dogs charged across the yard. They were bringing sacks full of just-made presents to all the sleighs lined up in a long, long row. The reindeer were harnessed and very excited. This was their big night.

But, inside the barn, it was very quiet.

Santa was wearing a brand-new suit. It was red, of course, a beautiful bright red because it was so new. He had loved the old suit – the most famous suit in the world – but it had ripped when he was bending over to put on his boots.

"You need a new suit," said Mrs Claus as she looked at Santa's underpants sticking out of the big hole at the back of his trousers.

"I need a new bum," Santa laughed. "This one's too big."

But Santa wasn't laughing now. The suit was supposed to make anyone who wore it or saw it happy, but it wasn't working.

Santa looked sad, and worried. It was Christmas Eve. And time was flying. He had a sleigh full of presents and a cranky old reindeer who wouldn't pull it. He should have been in New Zealand by now, climbing down and back up chimneys. And then there was Australia, and Papua New Guinea and Borneo, the Philippines, Japan and then China. It was night-time in all those places, the end of Christmas Eve. Millions and millions of sleeping children, all of them waking up in a few hours. And what would they find?

Santa was very worried.

If the presents weren't there, that would be the end of it. No presents, no Santa. That was how it worked. All those kids, all over the world, would stop believing in him. The magic would die and Santa would just be a very old man, with nothing left to do.

Santa was terrified.

"Come on, Rudi," he said. "We do it every year."

"No, man."

Rudolph was wearing his sunglasses and he had a bandanna tied around his antlers. (By the way, the bandanna had been given to him by a very old singer called Bruce Springsteen.)

"Oh, come on, Rudi," said Santa. "There are millions of children waiting for us. We have to give them their presents."

"But that's it, man," said Rudolph.

"That's all it's about these days. Presents, presents, presents. They're spoilt, man. The kids these days. They don't even say thanks."

"Yes, they do," said Santa.

"They don't mean it," said Rudolph.

"Don't be so cranky, Rudi," said Santa.

"Look, man, next year, maybe. It's a mid-life thing. I need a rest."

Rudolph lay down in the straw.

Santa patted him. Rudolph felt very hot and the world-famous nose was even redder than usual.

Santa knew.

"You have the flu, Rudi," said Santa.

"Sorry to let you down, man," said Rudolph.

"Don't worry," said Santa.

And Rudolph closed his eyes and slept. Santa put a blanket over his old friend's back. Then he went over to the sleigh. The presents were packed and ready, in sacks of different sizes. There were other sleighs already in the sky, all around the world, waiting to transfer more presents on to Santa's sleigh. All those children to be visited. All those countries, all those chimneys.

And here he was, stuck in the northern tip of Lapland, thousands of miles from where he should have been, on his way to New Zealand.

There were other reindeer. They were good, hard-working reindeer – but not good enough.

Rudolph was the strongest and the fastest. He was the best at reading the stars, at finding the way as he pulled the sleigh over the clouds. He was the best at parking on rooftops. He had the lightest hooves, the hooves of a ballet dancer. His hooves on slates never made a sound and they never went through straw roofs. And he sang all night as they flew from country to country. "Rudolph the coolest reindeer – you'll go down in his-TORY!"

Rudolph was the best.

But Rudolph was asleep and sick, and the famous nose looked like a tiny lighthouse in the middle of a very big ocean.

Santa patted Rudolph.

There was only one hope.

Santa knew what was what. He kept an eye on all the kids in the world, and their parents and pets. His elves sent reports to him. They wrote postcards, letters and e-mails. They sent carrier pigeons, Saint Bernard dogs and even an owl they borrowed from a kid called Potter. So, Santa knew: there was only one animal out there who could replace Rudolph. A dog. And that dog's name was – ROVER!!

CHAPTER FIVE
YOU CAN TAKE THE GLOVES OFF NOW, BUT LEAVE THE HAT ON BECAUSE IT'S STILL RAINING IN DUBLIN

ROVER!!

They looked at the dog asleep on his rug. The rug was in a shed behind the house. Rover's owners had put the rug there and left the shed door open so Rover would have somewhere to go when it was raining. It rains a lot in Ireland, so Rover had spent most of his life in the shed.

But that was fine with Rover.

Rover was fast, but so are a lot of dogs. He liked chasing things – cars, crows and helicopters – but so do most dogs. He pooed a lot, but so do all dogs. But what made Rover different was his mind. Rover had a brain the size of Africa tucked into a head the size of a baked potato. He pooed, yes, but then he sold the poo.

Does your dog do that?

Are you sure?

The fact is, very few dogs are brainy enough to sell their poo. But Rover sold his poo to the Gigglers, who then placed dollops of it on paths, to trap grown-ups who'd been mean to children. Rover also weed on the sides of cars, so that parents would pay their kids to wash the cars, and the kids always gave Rover ten per cent of the money. He'd been doing this for years and, like all dogs, he was a wee and poo factory. So Rover was a very rich dog.

Anyway, Rover was asleep on his rug. He loved lying on the rug because that was where he had his best ideas. It was a smelly old rug. It was so old, it was hardly there any more. In fact, the smell was the only solid bit of the rug left.

Rover snored.

"He's only pretending," said Jimmy. And Jimmy was right. Rover was pretending to be asleep.

THE RETURN OF
CHAPTER FOUR

Santa looked at the empty space in front of the sleigh, where Rudolph should have been.

He was getting more and more worried.

"What's keeping that elf?" he said to himself. "What's keeping that dog?"

He put his old head in his old hands. He was very cold and his back was beginning to hurt.

CHAPTER FIVE II

Rover kept his eyes shut.

When a gang of kids and an elf in a leather jacket called, looking excited and worried, that meant one of two things, trouble or work. And Rover wasn't in the mood for either of these things. He was a hard-working dog. But he was having a lazy day. He wasn't even scratching.

"Rover."

Rover's two eyes stayed shut.

"Bum-bum," said Victoria.

One of Rover's eyes opened.

"Rudolph's on strike? That's a pity."

And the eye closed again.

"But Santa wants you to pull the sleigh," said Robbie.

Rover's other eye opened.

"Do I look like a reindeer?"

The eye closed.

"Ah, come on, Rover."

"You can do it."

"Who are you?"

"Please, Rover."

"Bum-bum."

Rover knew: they weren't going to go away. His lazy day was vanishing in front of his closed eyes. Anyway, he liked kids. He hated to think that they wouldn't get their presents. And he'd always wanted to fly.

But Rover was a business dog.

"How much?" he said.

"Excuse me?" said the elf.

"How much will you pay me?"

"We were hoping you'd do it for nothing," said the elf.

"From the goodness of my heart?" said Rover. "That kind of thing?"

"Yes," said the elf.

Both of Rover's eyes opened.

"You want me to drag a sleigh full of presents and a fat lad in a red suit. And you want me to drag this sleigh all around the world? And you want me to do this for nothing?"

"Yes," said the elf.

The eyes closed, snap, like two smashed light bulbs.

"Night-night," said Rover. "Don't let the bugs bite."

And the elf took out his notebook.

CHAPTER FIVE'S BABY –
LITTLE CHAPTER SIX

"Let me see, let me see," said the elf. "Ah, yes."

He found the page he was looking for.

"I think," said the elf, "there's a girl dog in Galway called Lassie who'd be very interested in reading this."

One of Rover's eyes opened.

His girlfriend was called Lassie and she lived in Galway.

The elf continued.

"It says here," said the elf, "that a dog called Rover was seen holding paws with a girl dog *not* called Lassie when they went to see *My Dog Skip* at the Savoy last week."

Rover jumped up.

"When do we start?" he said.

"Good on yourself, Rover," said Robbie.

CHAPTER SIX –
THE TEENAGE YEARS

I don't want to be Chapter Six. I never asked to be Chapter Six. I'm not eating this muck. You don't understand my music. I want a car. Who said you could put my teddy bear up in the attic?

CHAPTER SEVEN

The elf closed his notebook with a happy snap.

"Let's get going," he said.

"Hold your horses, pal," said Rover. "If I go, I'll need help."

"What kind of help?" said the elf.

Rover pointed a paw at the children.

"That kind of help," he said.

"Great!" said Jimmy and Robbie, together.

"Children, delivering presents?" said the elf. "That's ridiculous."

"Listen, pal," said Rover. "Rover has one rule. In case of emergency, bring a child. This is a big emergency, right?"

"Right."

"Yeah. So, I'm bringing four children."

"But," said the elf.

"Great," said Rover. "I knew you'd see it my way. Right, kids," he said to Robbie, Jimmy, Kayla and Victoria. "Go home and get some warm clothes on."

The children ran.

"And, hey," said Rover. "Bring an atlas."

CHAPTER EIGHT

Robbie and Jimmy were dressed and ready.

Jimmy was wearing seven T-shirts, nine jumpers and four pairs of trousers.

Robbie was wearing nineteen T-shirts, three jumpers, a track-suit, three pairs of trousers and his bathing togs.

They were both wearing swimming goggles and *Liverpool* caps. They each had on a pair of their mother's mountaineering boots, stuffed full of slices of bread so they'd fit and stay warm.

And Robbie had his school atlas.

They were ready to go now, just waiting for Kayla.

They watched her coming down the stairs. Actually, she was sliding down the banister.

"Who are you?" she said, as she flew past them and hit the wall.

But she didn't hurt herself because she was wearing all the clothes she owned and some of her father's too. She had also made knee and elbow pads out of the nappies that she didn't need any more, because she had started using the potty.

She stood up and laughed.

They were ready to go.

Their mother, Billie Jean Fleetwood-Mack, was upstairs in the attic, practising her bungee-jumping.

"Mum!" called Robbie. "We're going out!"

"Where to?" they heard their mother say.

"Australia, Asia, Africa, Europe and North and South America!"

Suddenly, their mother was right in front of them, upside-down, her feet tied to a rubber rope. She'd just jumped out of the attic.

"That sounds nice," she said.

She was wearing a magnificent gold crash helmet.

"Look after your brothers, won't you?" she said to Kayla.

"Who are you?"

"Good girl," said Billie Jean. "Have a nice time."

And she was gone, back into the attic. They heard her helmet whacking the inside of the roof.

"Oh-oh," she said. "There go two more slates. Your daddy won't be happy."

Robbie, Jimmy and Kayla ran out of the house.

CHAPTER NINE

Meanwhile, in the house next door, Victoria's mother was helping Victoria to zip up her padded jacket.

Her mother's name was Tina.

"Goodness," said Tina. "You must have grown since we last put this jacket on you. Yesterday."

Tina had a beautiful voice. Everybody said so. Even the birds stopped singing to listen to her. The toilet pipes stopped gurgling, the cooker stopped cooking, the fridge warmed up whenever they heard Tina's voice. She worked at a radio station. She presented a programme especially for people who lived in Ireland but hadn't been born there. The programme was called *Pawpaw and Potatoes.*

USEFUL INFORMATION

The pawpaw is a small fruit, found in most tropical countries, and the potato is a small animal, found in Ireland. All young Irish people learn how to hunt potatoes. And potatoes are easy to hunt because they don't have legs, so they can't run away, and they don't have mouths, so they can't beg for mercy. The best way to hunt potatoes is with a weapon called a potato peeler. Wild potatoes can be found hiding among the vegetables in supermarkets. They can also be found in kitchens, where they nest in plastic bags, often in the bottom of fridges.

WARNING!

Organic potatoes are particularly dangerous. Be very careful when approaching them. And don't try hunting other wild animals, like lions and crocodiles, with a potato peeler.

Now, back to the story.

The programme was called *Pawpaw and Potatoes*. It was very popular. Everybody listened to it. Not just people who hadn't been born in Ireland. People who'd been born in Ireland listened too. People who had never been outside Ireland, not even for five minutes in a boat, not even for ten seconds for a swim – even these people listened to *Pawpaw and Potatoes*. Because they loved Tina's voice.

What was it like?
Her voice was like silk.

Silk doesn't have a voice.

Shut up! Her voice was like silk. It was like ice cream. It was like hot fudge. (A note for the adults: it was like a really good pint of Guinness.) It was like gravy. It was like the most beautiful music. It was like a baby laughing, like Bambi belching. Like a butterfly whispering, like a peacock farting. It was the beautiful voice of a beautiful woman, that was what it was. Does that answer your question?

Kind of.

Anyway, Tina had been looking everywhere for her best dress.

She zipped up Victoria's jacket and stood up.

"Did you see my best dress anywhere, Vicki-baa?"

"Bum-bum."

And Tina started laughing.

"You made a parachute with it?"

And she hugged Victoria and kissed the top of her head.

"Where do you get these ideas from?"

The telly turned itself on and off. It was showing off for Tina.

"Now," said Tina. "Have a nice time with Kayla. And don't go too far without asking permission first."

"Bum-bum?"

And Tina laughed again.

"Yes," she said. "You *may* go to Vietnam."

The telly changed channels and put the picture upside-down.

Victoria galloped through the kitchen to the back door.

"Hey, young one," said the cooker. "Is your ma coming in?"

"Bum-bum," said Victoria.

And she ran out of the door.

"Hey, lads," said the cooker. "Tina's coming!"

"Oh goodie," said the toaster.

"Is my hair OK?" said the fridge.

CHAPTER TEN

Meanwhile, Santa sat on a big log outside the reindeer's barn. He took his old head from his hands and looked up at the stars.

"Where are they?" he said.

CHAPTER ELEVEN

They were in Rover's garden.

The elf and Rover, Victoria and Kayla, Jimmy and Robbie. They were holding hands and paws in Rover's garden.

And, suddenly, they weren't. They weren't there any more.

They were standing beside Santa, up to their knees in snow.

How did that happen?

CHAPTER TWELVE

I'm not telling.
It's a secret.

CHAPTER THIRTEEN

Santa fell off the log.

But he jumped up again when he saw who had arrived.

"Boy, oh, girl," he said. "It's good to see you lot."

And then he did it. He gave his famous laugh.

"Ho ho ho!"

He hadn't laughed all day, but now his belly shook. It was the nicest, funniest sound they'd ever heard. His laugh made them laugh, and that made him laugh again, louder.

"HO ho ho!"

And he looked at Rover.

"The famous Rover," he said.

"The famous Santa," said Rover. "Where's the famous sleigh?"

"Inside the famous barn," said Santa.

And he looked at all the children.

"Who have we here?" he said.

"Four kids," said Robbie.

"So I see," said Santa.

"And an elf," said Jimmy.

"Who are you?" said Kayla.

"Nice to meet you, Kayla," said Santa.

"He brought them, Santa," said the elf, pointing at Rover. "It had nothing to do with me."

"The more the merrier," said Santa. "We need children tonight."

"Sorry to butt in here, lads," said

Rover. "But we have a sleigh here, a lot of presents, a lot of kids and not a lot of time."

He looked at Santa.

"So, big man," he said. "Why don't you hitch me up and we can hit the sky."

"Do you think you can do it?" said Santa.

"No sweat," said Rover. "The name's Bond. Rover Bond."

Santa put the blue harness over Rover's back.

"Is that too tight, Rover?"

"If it was too tight, pal, you'd know all about it. Are we ready to roll?"

The children climbed on to the sleigh.

"Is that Rudolph?" said Jimmy.

Rudolph was still asleep on the straw.

"He's having the night off," said Santa.

"He only works one night a year," said Rover. "But who's complaining? Are we ready?"

Rudolph opened his eyes.

"A dog pulling my sleigh!" he said. "Oh man, I'm going out of my mind!"

Santa covered Rudolph again, and patted his fur until he went back to sleep. Then he went over to Rover.

"Rover," he said.

"I'm listening," said Rover.

Santa spoke very quietly, so the children wouldn't hear him.

"I don't think we can do it," he said.

"Trust me," said Rover.

"I do trust you," said Santa. "It's not the speed. It's the chimneys, the bedrooms, the tricky stuff. I don't think we have the time."

"Guess what I have," said Rover.

"What?" said Santa.

"An idea," said Rover.

And that was how the lizards came back into the story.

CHAPTER FOURTEEN
THIS CHAPTER IS DEDICATED TO LIZARDS EVERYWHERE

Heidi kissed Hans's forehead.

"Thanks for the fly, Hans."

"Thanks for eating it, Heidi."

They were under the wet bush in the Macks' back garden.

And, suddenly, they weren't. The bush and the garden were gone and they were in Santa's barn.

How did that happen?

The answer is in the next chapter, on Page 170. Have a look. We'll wait for you.

They landed and bounced, and landed again.

"Wow," said Hans.

Then he saw Rover.

"Hi-dee-hi, Rover."

"Cold enough for you?" said Rover.

And Hans and Heidi suddenly noticed. It was cold. It was very cold.

How cold?

Did you ever stick your head in a freezer for ten minutes?

No.

Why not?

It's too cold.

Well, that was how cold it was. And Hans loved it.

"Nice," he said. "Very nice."

He rubbed his tummy on the ground.

"Very, very nice."

"Want to go where it gets even colder?" said Rover. "And help save Christmas at the same time?"

"Sounds cold," said Heidi.

"Sounds great," said Hans.

"Hop on board," said Rover.

"Okey-dokey, Rovie."

And Hans and Heidi jumped on to the sleigh. They landed on Victoria's lap, then hopped to the floor.

"Hi-dee-hi, kids."

"Bum-bum."

"Now," said Rover. "Let's break out of this place."

Santa stood up in the sleigh. He held the reins. He laughed – "Ho ho ho" – and shouted.

"Hey, ho! And away we go!"

And away they went.

Out of the barn door, into the yard, across the snow and up, pulled by the mighty Rover.

Up, up, up, and away. Into the air, into the sky. The elf waved goodbye.

Hang on.

Yes?

I know that reindeer can fly sometimes, but what about Rover? I've never seen a flying dog. Except for the one who was running after the plane and bit the wheel just when the plane was taking off. But what about Rover? He can't fly, can he?

Nine times out of ten, ninety-nine times out of a hundred, dogs can't fly. Take your dog to the park and say, "Bonzo, fly!" Bonzo will probably sit there and look back at you with one of those faces that says, "Sorry, chum, I'll chase your ball, I'll fetch your stick, I'll eat your shoe, I'll lick your granny's bald head, but I'm not going to be flying today." So, fair enough, dogs can't fly. But, *but*, BUT – when you're hanging around with Santa, you can expect magic things to happen, and that was exactly what was happening now. Magic. And good magic can never be explained.

Because it's magic. The real thing. Santa magic. Once-a-year magic. But, *but*, BUT – here's a genuine secret. This time the magic can be explained. The sleigh could fly, and Rover with it, because kids all over the world believed that it would. They believed it would fly, so it flew. The kids of the world kept the whole thing in the air. It was as simple as that. And that was what worried Santa so much. If the kids stopped believing, the sleigh wouldn't fly and Rover and Rudolph wouldn't fly. The sleigh, the sacks, the whole lot would tumble to the ground. No more magic, no more Christmas, and no more Santa. If they couldn't deliver the presents tonight, it would all be over. Kids would stop believing and

Christmas Day would become just another day of the year, a day off school, a day off work – nothing more. Rover was pulling more than a sleigh full of presents. He was pulling the future of Christmas. But he didn't know that. Only Santa knew.

Back to the story.

Rover didn't know how come he could fly. But he knew he would. When he jumped, when he felt his paws climbing the air like it was solid and friendly, he knew he was in the magic hands of Santa.

"I'm impressed!" he shouted over his shoulder.

"Nothing to it!" Santa shouted back. "Ho ho ho!"

Santa was glad there were kids on board. They made up for the loss of Rudolph. Rover flew beautifully, like an eagle with invisible wings.

Up, up they went.

They saw the world below, the

shining snow of northern Finland, the farmhouses, the lights from the kitchen windows lighting the snow.

Up, and away.

They saw snow-coated trees and the lights from the Spar supermarket in a small town called Muonio.

Up, up, up.

They saw the lights of Helsinki, the biggest city in Finland. And blocks of ice shining like giant, rolling diamonds in the Gulf of Finland. Up, up, into the clouds, and up.

CHAPTER FIFTEEN

Ha ha.
Fooled you.
It's a secret.

CHAPTER SIXTEEN

Up through the clouds they went.

"Ho ho ho."

And Rover picked up speed. They all hung on to the sleigh. They saw stars – millions of them – for a second, and then they were in clouds again. Then stars, more clouds, and stars, and nothing but stars. Glorious, beautiful, dancing, shooting stars. And others that stayed still and didn't shoot or dance at all.

And these were the stars that Robbie and Jimmy looked up at. These stars were their map, now that the land below was hidden by the clouds.

They were
looking for a
constellation.

What's a constellation?

Good question. A constellation
is a group of stars. For thousands of
years, people have been able to find
their way in the dark by following
these stars. The most famous constellation is probably the Plough. The
Plough is seven stars that look like an
old-fashioned plough.

"Look!" said Robbie.

He'd found the constellation they were looking for.

"The Teacher's Armpit," said Jimmy.

It was, indeed, the Teacher's Armpit. Thirty-seven stars that are shaped like a teacher's armpit. Seven stars make up the armpit and the other thirty make up the hair.

"Which way, lads?" Rover shouted back, over his shoulder.

"Follow that armpit, Rover," shouted Robbie. "South-east."

And that's where Rover brought

them, through the freezing sky over Estonia and Russia. His paws gripped the air like it was solid ground. He pulled them south, back into daytime. The stars disappeared and so did the clouds. Over the Caspian Sea and Iran. His snout cut through the air like it was warm butter. Over Pakistan and India.

They headed south. And they also flew east. They were over clouds again, so they couldn't see the countries and oceans below them. And then they couldn't see the clouds because Rover had pulled them into the night.

It was nine hours later, even though it was only twenty minutes since they'd flown out of the barn.

Jimmy and Robbie and Kayla and Victoria looked up for the next constellation.

Santa looked at his watch.

"Ho ho ho – I hope."

CHAPTER SIX –
THE ADULT

I hope they're wrapped up warm.
I hope they're wearing their safety
belts. I hope they have some sandwiches in case they get hungry on the
way. I hope they remember their
phone numbers in case they get lost. I
hope they don't make too much noise
when they're going over our house.

CHAPTER SEVENTEEN
THIS CHAPTER IS DEDICATED TO ALL THE FLIES THAT HAVE BEEN EATEN BY LIZARDS EVERYWHERE

And then they saw it.

"Who are you?"

They all spotted it at the same time, the second most famous constellation of them all.

"The Monkey's Bum!" said Robbie.

Forty-three stars shining happily. Twenty-four made up the bum and the other nineteen made up his underpants.

And the Monkey's Bum pointed them at New Zealand.

How?

Here was the trick. You had to look straight at it, for ten seconds without blinking. You had to stay absolutely still. So Rover stopped flying.

And they all stared.

For ten seconds.

Ten.

Seconds.

Ten.

Lo-ong.

Seconds.

And then it did it. The Monkey's Bum wriggled and did a little dance. Then stopped, pointing the way.

And they were off again.

"Follow that bum!"

"Hey ho, and away we go!"

South and east. Fast, fast, fast. Over the Indian Ocean, Thailand and Borneo. Faster than the fastest horse, the fastest car or snail, faster than the speed of sound and light, Rover dragged them over Papua New Guinea.

And down, through the clouds they went, as they flew over the Coral Sea. They could see ship lights on the ocean. Down, down, because soon they would be landing.

Soon the real work was going to start.

VERY OLD
CHAPTER SIX

We didn't have silly chapters like this when I was young. We had proper stories. And we didn't have pictures either. Where did I leave my teeth? And we didn't have televisions. Or food. Oh, there are my teeth. Biting my leg. Now, how did they get there?

I like the dog, though. And the children. And Santa, of course. Come to think of it, I did have a book with pictures. I had lots of books with pictures. And four tellys. And we did have food once. Now, where have they gone? Biting my other leg. I remember the days when teeth knew their place. In your mouth. That was where teeth went when I was young.

CHAPTER EIGHTEEN

And now they could see the lights of Auckland, the biggest city in New Zealand.

"Action stations, lads and lassies," said Santa. "Now, where's my list?"

Santa held on to Rover's reins with one hand and searched inside his red jacket and gave himself a good old scratch while he was at it.

"Where, where, where, where?"

"Where do we start, Santa?" said Jimmy.

"I don't know," said Santa.

He sounded worried.

"I can't remember."

And the sleigh started tumbling out of the sky.

CHAPTER NINETEEN

They all held on as the sleigh fell.
They heard Rover but they couldn't
see him.

"Who stole me wings!?"

He was under the sleigh.

The sleigh began to spin as it fell.

Santa knew what was happening.
When he'd said, "I don't know," the
kids had begun to wonder if he was
the real Santa. The real Santa would

never have said something like that. That was what they thought. But Santa was hopeless at stars and streets. He always had been. The stars and streets were Rudolph's department. Santa had a list of all the streets but he couldn't find it. And now the ocean was getting nearer and nearer as the sleigh continued to fall.

But he found it. Deep in his inside pocket – the kids were screaming and so were the lizards – he found the paper and pulled. And the kids saw the longest list they'd ever seen, a piece of paper that flapped in the wind and flew behind and above them like a tail.

And that was enough. They believed again – it was a Santa kind of list – and the sleigh and Rover stopped spinning and falling and the air stopped rushing past them. Rover could feel the air, like solid ground, under his paws again.

"No more messing," he said, over his shoulder. "We've got work to do."

"It's all the streets in alphabetical order," Santa told the kids as the sleigh dropped nice and slowly to the moonlit roofs of Auckland. "With all the children in each house. Abacus Street, Rover," he shouted to Rover. "I remember now. The second left after the lights down there. Pull up at the first roof, Rover."

Rover turned left on to the long, tree-lined street and, as if he'd been pulling and parking sleighs all his life, he brought the sleigh over to the first roof and dropped and slid and quietly, quietly stopped it on the slates. Not a scratch or a scrape or a bump.

"Nothing to it," whispered Rover.

Santa climbed out of the sleigh.

"Oh, my poor legs are stiff. Notice how warm it is?" he said.

"Who are you?" said Kayla.

"That's right," said Santa. "It's

summer down here. But keep all your clothes on in case you fall off a roof. Right," he said. "Let's get going."

And this was where the children, after years and years of getting presents from Santa, got the chance to pay him back.

DEAD
CHAPTER SIX

Hello!

It's nice up here.

Guess what I can see out of my window?

A big monkey's bum.

CHAPTER TWENTY
THIS CHAPTER IS DEDICATED TO NOBODY BECAUSE WE'RE IN A BIT OF A HURRY

Kayla lifted one of her jumpers and showed them what she'd hidden under it. Two of her mother's rubber bungee-jumping ropes, wrapped round and round her tummy. She started to unroll them.

"Who are you?" she said.

"Another brilliant idea from Kayla," said Jimmy.

They grabbed a rope and pulled. Kayla spun like a spinning top. She went whizzing to the edge of the roof but Santa caught her just in time.

"Who are you?"

"You're welcome," said Santa. "Now show me your idea."

Kayla tied one end of a rubber rope round her waist and handed the other end to Robbie.

"She needs the presents for this house," said Robbie.

Santa took five parcels from a sack and handed them to Kayla.

And then she jumped down the chimney.

Santa knew a good idea when he saw one.

"Ho ho ho," he laughed, very quietly. Robbie was holding on to the rope. He felt it tighten.

"Here she comes," he said, and a second later Kayla flew feet-first out of the chimney, and landed on Robbie's shoulders. She'd left the parcels down inside the house.

Meanwhile, Victoria tied one end of the second rope around her waist and Jimmy held the other end. Santa sorted out the parcels and began to feel very happy. But then –

"Oh, no," he said. "I forgot a parcel. Blocks for the baby."

"No problem," said Rover. "Right, lads," he said to the lizards. "Get down off the sleigh and show the man your stuff."

Hans and Heidi jumped on to the roof.

"It's getting crowded up here," said Jimmy.

Hans dropped his tummy to the roof.

"Hot," he said. "I think I'll change my name back to Omar."

And, immediately, the heat in the slates began to feel wonderful.

Omar spoke to Santa.

"Mister Claus. Do you remember, by any chance, do they get the presents under the tree or at the end of the bed in this house?"

"End of the bed," said Santa.

"And where's the babby's bed?" said Omar.

"Down the hall, first door after the toilet."

"Okey-dokey. Now, Mister Claus, could you please put the parcel on to the end of my tongue."

And, suddenly, Omar's tongue was right in front of Santa's nose. He held the parcel out and it stuck to the tongue like a stamp to a letter.

Omar jumped on to the chimney pot. And he fired his tongue down the chimney, down the hall, past the toilet, into the baby's bedroom. He wriggled his tongue, and the parcel fell off, neatly on to the end of the cot.

When his tongue came back up it held a plate with cheese sandwiches on it. And, suddenly, the plate was under Santa's nose.

"For you," said Omar.

And while Santa ate the sandwiches – but not the crusts – Rover brought the children and the lizards from roof to roof along Abacus Street. The street was done, all the presents delivered, before Santa had finished chewing the second sandwich.

CHAPTER TWENTY-ONE
THIS CHAPTER IS
DEDICATED TO KILLER
POTATOES EVERYWHERE

Blackhead Street.

Chlorine Street.

Dolphin Avenue.

Eagle Street.

They delivered the presents to every home in Auckland. And then they flew on to Christchurch and delivered to all the homes along the way. Omar and Heidi were able to flick their tongues down chimneys while the sleigh was moving and high above the chimneys.

By the way, Heidi's warm name was Sunshine.

Fluffy Street.

Gasp Street.

Hardware Avenue.

They were finished with Christchurch and all of New Zealand before

Santa had finished his three hundred and fifty-second sandwich.

"Where now?" said Rover. "Australia?"

"Nope," said Santa, and he sprayed breadcrumbs and little cheese bits into the sky. "Head north first, Rover. We have to beat the sun."

And as he said it, they could see the very tip of the sun, not even the tip – the light that was coming from the tip – rising, slowly, slowly, but rising steadily out of the ocean far away to the east.

"Oh oh," said Robbie.

"No problem," said Rover.

And up they flew – up, up and north.

CHAPTER TWENTY-TWO
THIS CHAPTER IS DEDICATED TO FLYING DOGS EVERYWHERE.

As they went north they stopped at every island on the way.

Norfolk Island.

New Guinea.

Guam.

And they parked on every roof that could take the weight of the sleigh.

When the roofs were made of straw Rover parked beside the house and Santa and the kids climbed in a window.

Every time they flew back into the sky there was another sleigh waiting for them, with full sacks to replace the ones they'd emptied. Rover didn't stop or slow down. The new sleigh flew beside him until the elves had thrown the new sacks on to the back of Santa's sleigh.

But the reindeer pulling the other sleighs couldn't keep up with Rover, not even the youngest reindeer, Nasu.

USEFUL INFORMATION

Nasu is the Finnish word for "Piglet". And, while we're at it, *Nalle Puh* are the Finnish words for "Pooh Bear", and *kakki* is the Finnish word for "poo". Lesson over, back to the story.

The children looked back and waved at the puffing reindeer as Rover charged north in his race against the sun – over forests and deserts, giant lakes and football pitches.

Slowly, slowly, the sun was creeping up out of the ocean, a tiny bit more every time Santa looked.

So he didn't look.

They flew to the far north of Siberia, and Rover ran on the spot so his paws wouldn't get frozen to the roofs.

And then they were heading south again.

Korea, North.

Korea, South.

Korea, in the middle.

Rover nearly crashed in Hong Kong. They flew down into fog and, suddenly, there was a glass skyscraper right in front of him, a few feet from his nose. He took a sharp turn left, and the side of the sleigh whacked the wall but didn't break the glass.

"Stupid place to put a building," said Rover.

The Philippines.

East Timor.

Australia took a bit longer than Japan. There were two reasons for this. First, it's bigger. Second, they were attacked by a flock of birds with machine guns.

A VERY ANNOYING COMMERCIAL BREAK

★ ★ ★ ★ ★ ★ ★

BRUSH YOUR TEETH WITH
DENTOFRESH TOOTHPASTE.

FAMOUS FOOTBALLERS BRUSH
THEIR TEETH WITH NEW,
IMPROVED DENTOFRESH.

DENTOFRESH – BRUSH YOUR
TEETH WITH IT AND GIRLS
WILL THINK YOU'RE COOL.

DENTOFRESH – BRUSH YOUR
TEETH WITH IT AND BOYS
WILL THINK YOU'RE COOL.

★ ★ ★ ★ ★ ★ ★

And now, back to the story.

CHAPTER TWENTY-THREE

THIS CHAPTER IS DEDICATED TO PEOPLE WHO USE DENTOFRESH EVERYWHERE

Jalopy Street.

Kangaroo Street.

They sat on a rooftop at the end of Lambchop Avenue, waiting for Santa for come up out of the last chimney. Rover's back was covered in snow, even though it was the middle of summer in Melbourne. It was the snow that had dropped on him in Siberia, thousands of miles away.

They were eating some of Santa's sandwiches, when they heard a voice behind them.

"Hands up."

They all turned.

It was a bird that was talking and he was pointing a machine gun at them. There were six other birds with him, all pointing machine guns at Robbie, Jimmy, Kayla, Victoria and Rover.

They were tall and orange, with red feathers standing up and waving on their heads. Their legs were pink, their claws were navy blue.

"Who are you?" said Kayla.

"We're the boorakooka birds," said the leader.

"That's us," said his friends.

"You didn't laugh," said the bird leader. "People used to laugh, every time we said boorakooka. Until we got the machine guns. Hand over the sack."

"No," said Jimmy.

"I have a machine gun. You don't have a machine gun. Hand over the sack."

"No," said Robbie.

"Hand it over."

"Bum-bum."

"It is *not* plastic," said the leader.

"Yes, it is."

"No, it isn't."

"Bruce!"

Santa's head was sticking out of the chimney.

The leader tried to hide the machine gun behind his back.

Santa climbed out of the chimney.

"I'm disappointed, Bruce," he said. "You said in your letter that you'd never point the machine gun at anybody."

"What machine gun?" said Bruce.

"Yeah," said the others. "What machine guns?"

"The ones behind your backs," said Santa. "Sticking up over your shoulders."

"They're only plastic, Santa," said Bruce.

"I know that, Bruce," said Santa. "I'd never give anyone a real machine gun for Christmas. But it's rude to point them."

"Sorry, Santa."

"That's OK, Bruce. Now, lads," he said to the boorakooka birds. "Go home to your nests and be asleep by the time I get there, or there'll be nothing for you this year."

And the boorakooka birds were gone. Just a few feathers floating in the air, that was all that was left of them. And, as Rover pulled the sleigh up to the sky, Santa leaned out – Robbie and Jimmy held him by his belt – and dropped presents into the boorakooka nests, in a huge eucalyptus gum tree at the end of Lambchop Avenue. They could see the machine guns hanging from the branches like Christmas decorations and, as they flew higher and higher, they could still hear the boorakooka birds snoring.

ANOTHER
COMMERCIAL BREAK

★ ★ ★ ★ ★ ★ ★

DO YOUR MAD COWS
HAVE BAD BREATH?

BRUSH THEIR TEETH WITH
FRESH-BREATH DENTOFRESH
IN THE NEW, IMPROVED TUBE.

★ ★ ★ ★ ★ ★ ★

CHAPTER TWENTY-FOUR

They went north, and back down south, and north again, and south. Like wipers on a rainy windscreen they swept across the world, with the sun always right behind them, getting a tiny bit nearer every time they looked.

Santa could feel the sun tickling the back of his neck, but it didn't make him laugh. It just made him more and more worried.

Bangladesh, all of Russia, Uzbekistan.

It was night-time in front of them and morning behind.

Iran, Oman, Libya.

Omar went back to Hans and back to Omar.

Finland, Bulgaria, Chad.

Sunshine went back to Heidi and back to Sunshine.

They saw lion packs asleep and packs of people coming home from parties.

Cameroon, Italy, Sweden.

They saw milkmen delivering milk and mad cows with bad breath dancing in the moonlight.

And when they came to Lagos, the biggest city in Nigeria, Victoria found the house of her grandparents.

THE BATTLE OF
THE PASTE

★ ★ ★ ★ ★ ★ ★ ★

BRUSH YOUR TEETH WITH
NEW TOOTHOFRESH AND
GIRLS WILL THINK YOU'RE
MUCH COOLER THAN
THEY DID WHEN YOU
USED DENTO-YUCKY-FRESH.

★ ★ ★ ★ ★ ★ ★

CHAPTER
TWENTY-FIVE

Victoria had never seen her grandparents' house before but it was easy to spot from the sleigh.

When she was a little girl, Victoria's mother, Tina, had climbed up on to the roof of the Mama and the Papa's house with a tin of paint and a big paintbrush. And she had painted this message in enormous letters:

Even after twenty years, the message was still loud and clear on the roof.

Her mother had told her so much about the house that Victoria had a perfect picture of it in her head – the blue windows, the red tin roof – and there it was now, right below her.

Rover swooshed down out of the sky over Lagos and landed on his velvet paws right beside the chimney. Jimmy held the bungee rope and Victoria jumped.

She landed in the big fireplace in the kitchen. Then she crept to the Mama and the Papa's bed. She had never seen them before, only in photographs. They were asleep and dreaming. She could tell: their dreams were sad. All of their children lived far away from Nigeria and they had never held and cuddled any of their grandchildren. Their dreams were full of empty rooms and voices belonging to children they couldn't see.

Victoria took two snow-domes out

of her jacket pocket. A snow-dome is a little glass dome full of water and thousands and thousands of plastic snowflakes. These were Dublin snow-domes. When you shook them the snow fell on to the River Liffey and the cacti that line the streets beside the river, and on to a sign that said, A PRESENT FROM DUBLIN.

Victoria put one dome under the Papa's pillow and the other one under the Mama's. She kissed them on their foreheads.

Then she crept back to the fireplace and pulled the rope.

ANOTHER COMMERCIAL BREAK

★ ★ ★ ★ ★ ★ ★ ★ ★

ONLY EEJITS USE
TOOTHOFRESH –

BRUSH YOUR TEETH
WITH CLINICALLY PROVEN
DENTOFRESH.

★ ★ ★ ★ ★ ★ ★ ★ ★

CHAPTER TWENTY-SIX

Above the clouds over Dublin, they met the sleigh that carried the Dublin presents, pulled by a reindeer called Paddy Last. They caught all the sacks that the elves threw at them.

Then Santa's sleigh came out of the clouds and they saw Dublin Bay below them. They all cheered. They were nearly home. They could see the city getting bigger and bigger.

But, suddenly, Robbie was worried. And, at the exact same time, Jimmy was worried.

"Hey, Santa," said Robbie.

"Ho ho ho," said Santa.

"We're not finished yet, are we?"

"No, no, no," said Santa. "We've all of Ireland, Iceland, Greenland, some other islands, and all the countries of North America, Central America and South America. And Hawaii."

"But," said Jimmy. "When we're in America, our parents will wake up because it will be morning here. Right?"

"Right," said Santa.

"And they'll see that we're not here," said Robbie. "And they'll be worried sick."

"And we'll be in trouble when we get home," said Jimmy.

"I never thought of that," said Santa. "What'll we do?"

"I don't know," said Santa. "I really don't know."

The sleigh wobbled and began to tumble.

"Who are you?" said Kayla.

"Yes!" said Santa. "Great idea, Kayla." And it was a great idea. Santa made the Mack parents and Victoria's parents sleep much longer than usual.

How?

Not telling.

The children landed on their own roofs and, while their parents slept, Victoria, Robbie, Jimmy and Kayla went down their own chimneys, and delivered their own presents to themselves. Robbie delivered Jimmy's and Jimmy delivered Robbie's.

"What did I get?" said Robbie.

"Not telling you," said Jimmy. "It's a surprise, ha ha. What did I get?"

"A doll, a drum, a kick in the bum and a chase around the table," said Robbie, "ha ha."

"Is Tina up yet?" said the toaster as Victoria sneaked through the kitchen.

"Does this shirt match my jacket?" said the fridge.

In only six minutes they were

finished with Dublin, and seven minutes later they'd done the rest of Ireland and they were flying out over the Atlantic Ocean, north towards Iceland. And while their children rode through a storm, their parents had the nicest dreams they'd ever had and slept through most of Christmas Day. Tina dreamed that she saw the Mama and the Papa lying in bed, at home in Lagos. They had big smiles on their sleeping faces. And Mister Mack dreamed about big, sexy cream crackers.

"My best-before date is the twentieth of October, 2004. Isn't that interesting?"

"I contain wheat flour, vegetable oil, salt and yeast. Isn't that interesting?"

And hundreds of miles away, Rover pushed into the storm.

"I wouldn't put a dog out in this weather," he muttered to himself.

"Ho ho ho," said Santa.

He looked behind him.

The sun was creeping up on them. Santa could put adults to sleep, but that kind of magic didn't work on the sun.

"Ho ho ho," said Santa.

CHAPTER TWENTY-SEVEN

Meanwhile, back in Lagos, the sun poked a finger through a gap in the curtains and woke the Papa and the Mama. They sat up together. They were feeling happy for the first time in years and years.

The Papa put his hand up to his forehead. He'd had a dream that his little granddaughter had kissed him, and now he could feel it, the kiss – it was still wet there in the middle of his forehead. (And it stayed there, wet and wonderful, for the rest of his long life.) And the Mama felt the kiss on her forehead too. She touched it, and cried happy tears. (And the kiss stayed there, a lovely tickle, for the rest of her long life, and even after.)

They looked at each other.

"Did you dream what I dreamed?" said the Mama.

"I think so," said the Papa.

And he felt something under his pillow. The snow-dome. He took it out and shook it and watched the snow falling on Dublin. And the Mama found her dome and shook it, too.

They held hands as they shook their domes.

"Dublin looks like a nice place," said the Papa.

"Yes," said the Mama. "Look, the air is full of sugar."

DENTOFRESH IS LOW IN
FLUORIDE AND SUGAR-FREE.
IT PROTECTS YOUR TEETH
AGAINST TOOTH DECAY.
ISN'T THAT INTERESTING?

IF YOU BRUSH YOUR TEETH
WITH TOOTHOFRESH, YOUR
TEETH WILL FALL OUT
AND YOU WILL DIE.
ISN'T THAT INTERESTING?

CHAPTER
TWENTY-EIGHT
THIS CHAPTER IS DEDICATED TO
SNOW-DOMES EVERYWHERE

Iceland, Greenland, Newfoundland.

They flew down the east coast of Canada, the U.S.A., across the sea to the Bahamas, Cuba and Jamaica. They hopped from island to island, dropping presents down chimneys and through open windows where there were no chimneys.

Brazil, Uruguay, Argentina.

In twenty-two minutes they delivered more than twenty million pairs of football boots to football-crazy kids. They went to the very tip of Argentina, to Tierra del Fuego, to the very last house before the South Pole.

And they flew back north, through the centre of South America.

Paraguay, Bolivia, Colombia.

The sun was crawling towards them. But they kept going, in the last minutes and seconds of darkness. Back up to the U.S.A.

New Mexico, Colorado, Wyoming.

The sun was beginning to light the snow on the Rocky Mountains, but they kept diving down and up the chimneys.

Alaska, the Yukon, British Columbia.

They flew south again, along the west coast of the Americas. And the sun peeked over the mountains. Suddenly, it was early morning.

"Please!" Santa roared at the sun. "Just give us five minutes!"

But the sun wasn't listening. Because the sun has no ears. Anyway, the sun wasn't moving – Earth was. But Earth doesn't have ears either, so Santa was wasting his time. And he knew. It was too late.

He let go of the reins and put his old head in his hands. He wasn't Santa any more. Because he'd failed. There were millions of kids who still hadn't got their presents, and they wouldn't be getting them now because they'd be waking up. And what would they find? Nothing. Nothing at the end of their beds, nothing under the Christmas tree. Santa had let them down. He was just a useless old man with nothing left to do. He waited for the sleigh to tumble out of the sky.

But it didn't.

It stayed up there.

Rover wasn't running, so they weren't moving. But they definitely weren't falling. Santa looked over the side of the sleigh, to check.

"What's wrong, Santa?" said Jimmy.

"Oh, kids, I'm sorry," said Santa.

"Why?" said Robbie.

"I'm not going to deliver the presents. All those poor children. They won't believe in me any more."

"Yes, they will," said Jimmy.

"Bum-bum."

"It's *you* we like, Santa," said Robbie. "The presents are just extra."

"Yeah," said Jimmy. "And, anyway, we already got our presents, so we don't care that much."

And the others nodded, even Hans and Heidi.

Rover had unhitched himself and he now climbed into the sleigh.

"Is this a private conversation, or can any dog join in?" he said.

"What do you think, Rover?" said Santa.

"About what, exactly?" said Rover.

"About not delivering the rest of the presents."

"Who says we won't?" said Rover.

"But it's too late," said Santa. "They won't believe in me any more."

He pointed at the sun.

"I don't get it," said Rover. "One of the kids down there wants a doll. Is it a better doll because you deliver it in the dark?"

"Well. No."

"So, what's the problem?" said Rover. "Give the poor kid her doll."

"In daylight? Now?"

"I'm not hanging around till night-time, pal," said Rover. "Think about it. All those kids wake up. Boo-hoo. No presents. Then you fall down the chimney with the presents. And you're worried that they won't believe in you? Cop on."

Nobody said anything for a while, then —

"Ho ho ho," said Santa.

"Now you're talking," said Rover.

THE RETURN OF DEAD
CHAPTER SIX

Guess what I just saw flying past my window?

A dog pulling a sleigh full of kiddies and lizards.

Ooh, I like it up here.

Hey, Elvis, come over here and look at this.

CHAPTER
TWENTY-NINE

They made it.

Every house and hut and flat and apartment and trailer and caravan and hospital and igloo – every home and building that had a child in it – they delivered the presents to them all. Kids laughed and grown-ups fainted when Santa fell down the chimney.

They were nearly stopped in Mexico, when they met the Walking Poo of Guadalajara. This was a huge poo that stood on people, getting them back for all the poos that people stand on every day. But, just in time, they saw the giant yucky foot coming down on them, and they legged it, back to the sleigh, and up and away.

"Come back here, *amigos*, till I stomp on yis," yelled the Walking Poo.

"Happy Christmas, Poo!" they yelled back as they flew on to Mexico City.

And they were nearly stopped when Rover crashed in Honolulu. He saw a lovely-looking collie below them and he watched her as she sniffed a gate. And he kept watching as he flew past – straight into a huge palm tree.

"Who put that there?" said Rover as they fell through the branches, to the ground.

They weren't hurt.

"Sorry, lads," said Rover.

"You were blinded by love, Rovie," said Hans.

"If you say so, pal," said Rover.

Kayla and Victoria fixed the sleigh.

How?

They put the runners back on it.

How?

With super-glue.

What super-glue?

Shut up.

And they were up and away again.

To Samoa, Phoenix Island and the very last stop, Midway Island.

To the last house.

On the very end of the very last street.

Number 27, Zulu Street.

They stood back and let Santa climb down the last chimney.

BATTLE OF THE PASTE II

★ ★ ★ ★ ★ ★ ★ ★ ★

DO YOUR TEETH GET DIRTY
WHEN YOU CLIMB UP AND
DOWN CHIMNEYS ALL NIGHT?
USE DENTOFRESH AND —

DON'T! USE TOOTHOFRESH.
IT'S MUCH BETTER.

NO, IT ISN'T !

YES, IT IS!

PUSH OFF, BOTH OF YOU.

WHO ARE YOU?

NEW, CLINICALLY
TESTED MINTOFRESH!

OH, NO! IN A NEW,
IMPROVED TUBE! AAAAH!

CHAPTER THIRTY

Santa's head came out of the chimney, and the rest of Santa followed.

He looked at them and smiled.

"Home," he said.

"Good on yourself, Santa," said Robbie.

"Over the North Pole, Rover," said Santa. "It's the quickest way."

"Now you're talking," said Rover.

Back into the air they went, and Rover turned and headed north and east.

Home.

They were tired and happy. They huddled together and stayed warm.

Home.

They flew over mountains and valleys made of ice, the most beautiful landscape on earth, but they were too tired to look.

Home.

CHAPTER THIRTY-ONE

And here they were.

Flying out of the clouds over Dublin. The cacti that line the streets of the city saw them and waved.

"Well done," said a cactus.

"Medium rare!" said his girlfriend beside him.

They landed just as their parents were waking up.

Santa hugged them and climbed back into the sleigh.

"What's the story?" said Rover.

"Lapland, please, Rover," said Santa.

"Fair enough," said Rover. "But it's going to cost you."

"How much?" said Santa.

"Three quid," said Rover.

"One," said Santa.

"Two," said Rover.

"One fifty," said Santa

"One seventy-five," said Rover.

"One seventy-one," said Santa.

"One seventy-four."

"One seventy-two."

"One seventy-three."

"Done," said Santa. "Ho ho ho."

"Plus ten per cent service charge," said Rover. "Ho ho ho."

And he ran, and lifted himself on to the air. And, before the parents came out to the garden, the sleigh and Rover and Santa – "Ho ho ho!" – were gone.

"Bye-dee-bye, kids," said Hans.

"Come along, Hans," said Heidi.

And they wriggled in under their

bush just before Mister Mack arrived.

"Up already?" said Mister Mack.

What Mister Mack didn't know was, it was four o'clock in the afternoon. The day was nearly over.

"What did Santa bring you?" said Billie Jean.

"Eh."

Jimmy looked at Robbie.

"Eh."

Robbie looked at Jimmy.

"Who are you?" said Kayla.

"You didn't open them yet?" said Billie Jean.

"Bum-bum," said Victoria.

"You wanted to say Happy Christmas to each other first?" said Billie Jean. "Isn't that sweet?"

"Ah, there you are, Vicki-baa."

It was Tina.

"Hey, lads," said the bush. "Tina's in our garden."

"Oh, wow," said the shed. "Is my roof OK?"

She was with Celestine, Victoria's father. Celestine looked up at the sky.

"Notice anything?" he said.

They all looked.

"It isn't raining," he said.

And he was right. For the first time in four months it wasn't raining.

"And look!"

In Lagos, the Papa and the Mama sat in bed and shook their snow-domes.

And in Dublin, it had started to snow.

"Brilliant!" said Jimmy. "We can make a snowman."

Robbie put his hand out and caught a snowflake. Then he licked it off his hand.

"It isn't snow," he said. "It's sugar."

"Brilliant!" said Jimmy. "We can make a sugarman."

They all ran around the garden, the kids in their padded-up clothes and the adults in grown-up jammies and T-shirts. They chased and laughed and caught the falling sugar in their open hands and mouths.

The sugar was general all over Ireland. It was falling on every part of the dark central plain, on the treeless hills, falling softly upon the Bog of Allen. It was falling, too, on the baldy heads of little Irish men and women and on the mad cows that use new, improved Mintofresh.

Back in the garden, the kids were building a sugarman.

And what about their magic night with Santa? They'd forgotten all about it. When Santa had hugged them, he'd taken back their memories of the night. They remembered, but only in their dreams. Sometimes Jimmy would dream about flying through the clouds, and Kayla would bungee-jump into warm kitchens, and Robbie would fly over lion packs, and Victoria would kiss the foreheads of the Mama and the Papa in Lagos.

And, maybe because of that magic night, as they grew older and became teenagers, then grown-ups, they still did childish things, even when they became very old. Jimmy often farted under the bedclothes and giggled, even when he was eighty-three. Kayla rubbed her nose on other people's shoulders and left a trail of snot on them, even when she was thirty-eight. Robbie often rang on doorbells and ran away, even when he was ninety-one. And Victoria? She was still jumping out of upstairs windows when she was a hundred and twenty-seven.

ANOTHER ENDING

If you thought that ending was a bit soppy, here's a different one.

And maybe because of that magic night, as they grew older and became teenagers, then grown-ups, they got madder and madder and more and more crazy. Jimmy became the most famous bank robber in the world. He didn't just rob the money. He took the buildings as well. Kayla became a scientist and invented a way of bringing dead volcanoes back to life.

And she invented a microwave that could turn nuggets back into chickens. All over the world, mothers and fathers had heart attacks when they opened their microwave doors. Robbie became the president of Ireland and went all over the world meeting very important people. But that's not all he did. When he was having dinner with the very important people he'd climb in under the table and tie their laces together. Sixteen presidents and twenty-seven prime ministers broke their legs while Robbie was the president, and no one ever caught him. And Victoria? She was still throwing people out of upstairs windows, even when she was two hundred and twelve.

ANOTHER ONE

If the last ending was a bit too violent and crazy for you, and if you're a parent and you're worried about letting your child read the book, here's a different one.

And, maybe because of that magic night, as they grew older and became teenagers, then grown-ups, they all became fine, respectable citizens. Jimmy always lifted the toilet seat before going for a wee and never, ever did it on the floor – because it's very unhygienic and unfair to people who don't like sitting on wet toilet seats. Kayla always put her sweet papers in the bin and never, ever threw them on the ground – because it's a bad thing to do and it makes a mess and ruins the environment and it stops tourists from coming to Ireland to spend their money. Robbie always brushed his teeth and never, ever just wet the toothbrush and pretended that he'd brushed them – because that's a sneaky thing to do and it upsets the grown-ups and you'll need your teeth all your life, for eating food and biting sellotape. Robbie's motto was, "My teeth are my best friends." (By the way, he used new, clinically tested Mouthofresh, in the new, improved digital tube.) And Victoria? She was still closing upstairs windows in case someone fell out, even when she was three hundred and seventy-six.

THE REAL ENDING

After they'd made the sugarman, they went inside and had their dinner. And it was very nice, especially the spuds and gravy.

THE MESSAGEY BITS

All good stories have messages, and this one has eight of them. Here they are:

1. If your name is Dermot and you live in Sligo, your mammy says you're to hurry home because your dinner is getting cold.

2. If you're alone in the kitchen but you think there's someone looking at you, it might just be the fridge.

3. If you're standing at an upstairs window and a girl called Victoria runs into the room, be careful.

4. For healthy gums and that tingling fresh-breath feeling, use new improved Smilofresh, with new harmless fluoride.

5. If your name is Dermot and you live in Sligo, your mammy is getting very annoyed.

6. If you hear strange noises coming from your roof, it's probably Rover, practising for next Christmas.

7. If you're a fly and you live in a country that has no lizards, you should still have your passport ready – just in case.

8. If your name is Dermot and you live in Sligo, your mammy says she's given your dinner to the cat and it serves you right and you'll just have to make do with a bowl of cornflakes.
   So there.

THE END

Hey, pal.
Oh, yes. Sorry Rover. I nearly forgot.

9. If you're a fine-looking collie and you live in Honolulu, Rover says *Aloha*.

THE END

Hey, Dermot. Your mammy isn't angry any more and when she said that she'd given your dinner to the cat she was telling a fib. It's lovely – chicken and spuds – and there's ice cream after. And, by the way, she has chocolates and other great stuff hidden in her handbag.

BIBLIOGRAPHY

If you liked this book, here are some more you might enjoy.

Rover Saves Easter
(Hound Dog Press)

Rover Saves Friday Afternoon 2
(Hound Dog Press)

Tuesdays with Rover
(Dog Poo Philosophy Press)

The Dog with the Golden Gun
(Armed Hound Books)

*Leave All Your Money to Your Dog: A Self-Help
Guide for Rich People Who Are Dying*
(Dog Poo Philosophy Press)

*Yo! I Bit Eminem's Leg!: The Confessions
of a Dogsta Rapper*
(Snoop Dog Books)

A Is for Ankle, B Is for Bite It: A Canine Dictionary
(Dogford University Press)

Rover Saves Easter Again
(Hound Dog Press)

How to Sniff Friends and Influence People
(Dog Poo Philosophy Press)

Rover Copperfield
(Kennel Classics)

All of these exciting titles are
available from *www.dogpoo.ie*
"Putting the woof back into reading."

Roddy Doyle

The Meanwhile Adventures

Illustrated by Brian Ajhar

■■ SCHOLASTIC

To Rene'e
R. D.

To Kevin, Jake and Eric
B. A.

CHAPTER ONE

Once upon a time there was a little girl who lived in a house made of gingerbread—

Boring.

There was once a little girl called Kayla Mack, and she lived in a house made of—

Still boring. Start again.

OK.

A little girl called Kayla Mack lived in a—

Still boring. Start again. And this is your last chance.

OK. One, two, three —

Kayla Mack stood on the cat's head. She pressed her foot on the head until it squeaked. She pressed three times and ran out the back door of her house. By the way, the house wasn't made of gingerbread. And, by the way, the cat squeaked because it was plastic. The squeak was a signal to her friend, Victoria.

How's that, so far?

Not bad, so far. Continue.

On her way out the door she met her father, Mister Mack. He was carrying a machine gun.

"Who are you?" said Kayla.

"It's not a machine gun," said Mister Mack. "It's a saw. I just invented it."

"Who are you?"

"I know it looks like a machine

gun," said Mister Mack. "But it's a saw. Look. I'll show you how it works."

But Kayla wasn't interested. Once you've seen one machine gun, you've seen them all. She kept running.

CHAPTER TWO

Mister Mack was happy.

But Kayla wasn't.

Because she was stuck in a hedge.

"Who are you!"

The hedge was a big hairy one, between the Macks' garden and her friend Victoria's garden. There was a hole in the hedge and it was a good shortcut, if you could find the hole. And that was the problem. Kayla had missed the hole. She was right beside it, but up to her knees in leaves and little branches that grabbed at clothes and wouldn't let go.

"Who are you!"

Two lizards lived in the hedge, and some budgies who'd escaped from the pet shop – they pretended they were sparrows – and a rat that only ate fresh vegetables.

Boring.

He used to eat everything. In his life, so far, he had eaten thirty-six dead animals, and three live ones. He'd eaten 365 different types of biscuits. He'd eaten car tyres, crisps and half a pedestrian bridge.

But not any more.

"I never liked being a rat," he was telling Kayla, although she wasn't listening.

She was shouting for Victoria to come and rescue her.

"Who are youuuuuu!"

CHAPTER THREE

Mister Mack was happy. And that was nice, because it was a long time since Mister Mack had been happy. Seventy-three days, exactly. If you counted back seventy-three days – and Mister Mack did it all the time – you came to the day when Mister Mack lost his job in the biscuit factory.

"Nobody's eating biscuits any more," said his boss, Mister Kimberley. "They're all too healthy."

They were standing beside Mister Mack's desk. There was a set of weighing scales on the desk, a photograph of his family and a big bronze fig-roll:

ALL-IRELAND BISCUIT-TESTING CHAMPION – 2004.

"Nobody's eating biscuits any more," said Mister Kimberley. "Even the rats have stopped eating biscuits."

Mister Mack was a biscuit tester. The factory made 365 different types of biscuits, a biscuit for every day of the year. And Mister Mack tested them all. He measured and weighed them. He crumbled and smelled them. And he tasted them. That was his favourite part of the job. He bit with his teeth, but his tongue did most of the work. And Mister Mack's tongue was the best in the biscuit business. He could tell if a biscuit had gone even ten minutes past its best-before date. He could tell if the jam in the middle wasn't jammy enough, if the chocolate on the outside wasn't milky enough. Mister Mack was the best biscuit tester in Ireland.

"I'm sorry," said Mister Kimberley. "But we have to stop making the biscuits."

"All of them?" said Mister Mack.

"No," said Mister Kimberley. "We're keeping the cream crackers."

"Oh no!" said Mister Mack.

"One a day," said Mister Kimberley, "we're going to stop making the biscuits. Until we're left with just the good old cream crackers."

"We're healthy and nutritious, and sneaky and malicious," said the cream cracker in Mister Mack's head, the one that always spoiled his daydreams. "Isn't that interesting?"

Mister Mack hated the cream crackers.

"Does that mean I'm fired?" he asked Mister Kimberley.

"No, no," said Mister Kimberley. "Don't worry. We want you to test the cream crackers."

"No way!" said Mister Mack.

He picked up his bronze fig-roll and walked out of the factory and all the way home, because he couldn't remember where he'd parked his car. In fact, he was so upset, he couldn't remember if he owned a car. (Interesting fact: he didn't.)

But Mister Mack wasn't the kind of man who stayed upset for long. By the time he got home — it took him four hours — he'd decided that, if he couldn't be a biscuit tester, then he'd be something else instead.

He walked in the back door. His wife, Billie Jean Fleetwood-Mack, was standing on the kitchen table. She'd just jumped there, from the top of the fridge.

"I'm going to become an inventor," said Mister Mack.

"What kind of inventor?" asked Billie Jean.

"A mad one," said Mister Mack.

CHAPTER FOUR

All that had happened seventy-three days before. Meanwhile, Kayla was still stuck in the hedge.

"Have you any idea how many calories there are in a fig-roll?" asked the rat.

Kayla yelled.

"Who are you!"

Where was her friend, Victoria? What was keeping her?

"It's shocking," said the rat. "All those calories, going straight to my hips. And there was me in that factory eating away, for years."

"Tweet tweet," said a budgie. "Will you listen to that eejit."

"Tweet tweet," said his chum. "I'm going back to the pet shop."

"Last one back is a chicken nugget, tweet tweet."

"Chicken nuggets?" said the rat. "Those things should be banned. The chickens of the world should be ashamed of themselves."

"Who are you!"

Kayla was four years old and she could say a lot more than "Who are you?" but, because everyone she knew loved her so much, they understood exactly what she meant, so she usually didn't bother saying anything else. But she could when she wanted to.

Here is an example of something that Kayla could say:

"If you don't shut up, I'll break your head."

She said it now to the rat.

"Charming," said the rat.

"Who are you!!"

Where was Victoria?

CHAPTER FIVE

Meanwhile, Mister Mack walked into the sitting room. His two sons, Robbie and Jimmy Mack, were in there. They were on the floor, playing a game called War.

Rules: War is a game for two or more players. Players shout "War!" at each other until they become bored or hungry or are bursting for a wee, and leave the room. The last player in the room is the winner. Also, the game ends if someone else walks into the room. There is no time limit.

(Interesting fact: The longest game of War has been going on for more than twenty-eight years, in Tipperary. The two remaining players, the O'Hara twins, Eddie and Kenny, are now thirty-nine. They haven't slept since 1976.)

Anyway, Mister Mack rushed into the room. (And the War ended.)

"Look, lads," he said.

"Nice machine gun, Dad," said Jimmy.

"It's not a machine gun," said Mister Mack. "It's a saw. Look."

He put a piece of wood against the wall. He stood back and pointed his saw at the wood.

"Now, lads. Watch."

The air was suddenly full of wood chips, and noise.

The noise stopped. Mister Mack looked pleased.

"See?"

He pointed at the wood, which was

now two pieces of wood.

"I sawed it."

"Fair enough, Dad," said Robbie. "But you smashed the windows as well."

"And the door and the sofa and the picture of Granny," said Jimmy.

"Oh," said Mister Mack.

He looked around the room. Some of the padding from the sofa had landed on his head.

"Ah, well," he said.

He looked at the wood again.

"It just needs fine tuning."

He patted the saw, and smiled. At last, he had invented something that would make him some money. He had been an inventor for only seventy-three days but, already, Mister Mack had invented lots of things. Mousetraps that tickled the mice until they promised to leave the house. A special brush for getting fluff off duvet covers—

Boring.

A bomb that made big men poo. A fridge that said "Go to the shops" when you opened the door and it was empty. Little batteries to put into bigger dead batteries. A machine that turned green recycling bins into plastic bags. And the toilet was really special: you could wee and wash your hands at the same time. These were all Mister Mack's inventions. The house was full of them, and they were all great.

But nobody wanted them. And Mister Mack was running out of money. The fridge said "Go to the shops!" before he even touched the handle.

The saw was Mister Mack's last chance.

He knew it would work. He just needed a little more time to make it perfect, and a little more money to keep them going.

He smiled again at Jimmy and Robbie.

"I'm off to the bank," said Mister Mack.

"Oh oh," said Robbie.

"Do you want to come with me?" asked Mister Mack.

"Are you sure about this, Dad?" said Jimmy.

"Yes," said Mister Mack. "We'll be back in plenty of time for dinner."

"But," said Robbie.

"But," said Jimmy.

"But," said Mister Mack, "the bank will be closed if we don't hurry up. Come on, boys."

Mister Mack went out the front door, and Jimmy and Robbie ran after him.

CHAPTER SIX

Meanwhile, Victoria rescued Kayla.

How?

Good question. She did it with another of Mister Mack's inventions. A hook for pulling children out of hedges.

"Who are you?"

"Batteries included!"

Victoria was four, the same age as Kayla. The exact same age. They were born at the same moment, in the same hospital, in the same ward, but not in the same bed. And now they lived next door to each other. "Batteries included" weren't the only words that Victoria could speak, but because everybody who loved her always knew what she meant, she usually didn't bother saying anything else.

"Who are you?"

"Batteries included!"

Here's what they meant:

KAYLA: What kept you?

VICTORIA: Well, I couldn't hear you because my mammy was singing and then she stopped and I heard you but I was a bit hungry so I made a ham and banana and bread sandwich, and then I had to put my jigsaw back in the box and then I couldn't find my boots and I found them in the fridge and here I am and stop complaining and grab the hook.

Kayla leaned out and took the hook. She put it under the belt of her trousers. A rope went from the hook to the back of Victoria's bike. Victoria was on the bike, on top of her slide. She put her foot on the pedal and pushed. She cycled down the slide and Kayla flew out of the hedge. She landed behind Victoria, and Victoria kept pedalling. And she was doing fifty miles an hour, right through a flock of lost budgies.

"Holy Mother of God, what was that — tweet tweet?"

And she was going even faster when they got to the front gate.

"Who are you!"

"Batteries included!"

The speed limit is thirty miles an hour, on the road, but the bike was doing sixty, on the path. Victoria turned right before they reached the road, and the bike headed straight towards a lady and her daughters. There were three daughters, and they were all the same age.

"Oh, good gracious!" said the lady.

"Oh, good gracious!" said the first triplet.

"Oh, good gracious!" said the second triplet.

"Oh, stop copying *her* all the time!" said the third one.

The lady and two of the triplets jumped out of the way, on to the road, which was safer because the trucks and cars were only doing thirty. The third triplet jumped on to the garden wall, which was even safer because the wall was doing nothing.

Kayla and Victoria went in one direction, so they didn't see Mister Mack or Robbie or Jimmy, because they were going in the other direction.

Jimmy and Robbie heard the triplets.

"Did you see that?"

"Did you see that?"

"I'm much more interested in *this*!"

But they didn't look back to see the triplets or to see what this was.

(Interesting fact: *this* was a slug, and it was wearing a crash helmet, and it was charging very slowly across the path.) They'd seen the triplets three times already that day. They had to run to keep up with Mister Mack. He was very excited. He took the saw off his shoulder and swung it in the air.

"Hello, Missis O'Janey," he called to one of his neighbours.

Missis O'Janey was in her garden. She was bending down, looking at a slug with a crash helmet. She looked up, with a smile ready for Mister Mack – and she saw the saw. She screamed and ran back into her house.

But Mister Mack didn't notice. He was now looking at all the other people who were screaming and running away. The street was full of them. People screaming, slugs with crash helmets.

"Interesting," said Mister Mack.

He walked on one of the slugs.

No, he didn't.

He carefully stepped over it and—

Boring.

His foot landed on two others and, if it hadn't been for their crash helmets, they'd have been squashed.

"It just goes to show you," said a slug. "You should never go out without your crash helmet."

"Yes," said his friend. "But I still wish mine was red."

Mister Mack walked on.

The bank was straight ahead. He could see the big sign – BRING ALL YOUR MONEY OVER HERE – on the roof. The bank was right beside the building that used to be the pet shop, Cuddly Pets. Cuddly Pets had closed down the day before because of the budgie shortage, and it was now a butcher shop, Tasty Meat.

Mister Mack passed a flock of budgies. They were on the path, outside Tasty Meat.

"Where's the pet shop, tweet tweet?" asked a budgie.

"I don't know," said another budgie. "And I'm not going in there to find out, tweet tweet."

But Mister Mack didn't notice the budgies.

He was at the door of the bank when Jimmy and Robbie caught up with him. They wanted to save their father, because they loved him—

Boring.

But what they didn't realize was, they had just saved the world.

How?

I thought you were bored.

Tell me.

OK.

CHAPTER SEVEN
HOW JIMMY AND ROBBIE MACK
SAVED THE WORLD

They nearly stood on a slug.

CHAPTER EIGHT

Mister Mack pushed the door of the bank and—

Hey!

Yes?

What about Robbie and Jimmy saving the world and all that?

OK. Here goes –

THE SLUGS OF DUBLIN

The slugs of Dublin had decided to take over the world. They arranged a meeting in a hotel, but it took some of them so long to get there that the hotel had been knocked down and was a car park by the time they arrived. So, they had their meeting in the car park.

"Hands up who wants to take over the world?" said the leader.

"We don't have hands," said a slug.

"What's the world?" said another.

"The world's a big, round place," said the leader. "And just raise your feelers instead."

The leader counted the feelers.

"That looks like everybody in favour," he said.

"No," said a slug. "Mine isn't up. It just looks like it is."

"OK," said the leader. "All except one are in favour of taking over the world."

The slugs cheered.

"Right," said the leader. "Let's get out there and kick some human posterior. But first, everybody has to wear crash helmets. There are millions of feet and tyres out there."

"I want a red one!" shouted a slug.

"There's only one red one," said the leader, "and I'm having it."

"Not fair!" said the slug.

"Are we ready?" said the leader.

"Yessss!" thousands of slugs shouted.

"Charge!"

And, twenty-seven days later, the slugs were still charging.

"No legs good, two legs bad! No legs good, two legs bad!"

And they were charging across the path when Mister Mack stood on two of them. And then, as they watched Mister Mack's feet move away, Jimmy

and Robbie very nearly stood on them.

"No legs good – God!"

Jimmy's lace whacked a crash helmet. The sole of his trainer looked like a slowly moving cliff beside them, right against them. They watched it lift and slowly fall back toward them.

"Ah here," said a slug. "I'm going home."

"Me too," said his pal.

The other slugs watched their friends turning back, and most of them followed.

"Come back!" yelled the leader.

"Not unless you give me the red one," said a slug.

"No way," said the leader.

And the slugs kept going. The world was still safe for humans, all because of Jimmy's and Robbie's big feet.

That wasn't very good.

Dead and badly injured slugs littered the battlefield. People walked knee-deep in slug guts. Budgies pecked at the dead and mutilated bodies. A dying slug handed his buddy his watch.

"Make sure my wife gets this," he said. "And tell the kids to do their homework every night."

"How many kids have you?" asked his friend.

"Four hundred and seventy-two."

"Will I tell them each individually, or will all together do?"

"Whatever," said the slug.

His eyes closed, and opened.

"It's a pity you don't have arms," he said. "Then I could have died in them."

"Ah, well," said his friend.

The slug's eyes closed, stayed closed, then opened.

"D'you know what?" he said. "I don't feel too bad now."

Boring.

Then a triplet stood on him.

CHAPTER NINE

Mean . . .

while, Mister Mack walked into the bank, Kayla and Victoria were robbing a different bank.

Really?

No. Kayla and Victoria were robbing the supermarket, but that's a very different story.

What did they rob?

I don't have time to tell you, but it was delicious and the chocolate came off in the wash.

Mister Mack walked into the bank. It was full, but suddenly, there was plenty of space in front of him. He walked right up to the woman behind the counter.

"Good morning," said Mister Mack. The woman didn't answer.

"That's a bit rude," said Mister Mack to himself.

And he noticed something. Her hands were sticking up in the air. Mister Mack looked around. More people had their hands in the air. In fact, everybody had their hands in the air.

"Aha," said Mister Mack to himself.

"It must be stick-your-hands-up-in-the-air day. For charity."

"I want to talk to the manager, please," said Mister Mack to the woman behind the counter.

He held up the saw.

"I think he'll give me some money when he sees this," he said. "What do you think?"

"Yes," said the woman.

"How much do you think he'll give me?" said Mister Mack.

"As much as you want," said the woman.

"Great," said Mister Mack. "It'll be easier than I thought. Will he talk to me, do you think?"

"I'm sure he will."

"Great," said Mister Mack. "Because the last time I asked him for money, he told me to get lost and to stay out of his bank."

"I don't think he'll say that this time," said the woman.

"Great," said Mister Mack. "I told him I had an idea that would kill him. But I don't think he was listening."

Robbie and Jimmy saw the manager, Mister Meaney, come out of his office behind the counter. And they heard a siren. And another siren. And more sirens.

"There must be a fire somewhere," said Mister Mack.

"Yes," said the woman behind the counter.

Mister Meaney walked slowly to the counter.

"Good morning, Mister Eh —"

"Mack," said Mister Mack.

"Ah yes," said Mister Meaney. "Good morning, Mister Mack."

"Good morning, Mister Meaney," said Mister Mack.

He pointed the saw at Mister Meaney, and Mister Meaney put his hands in the air. The sirens outside got louder and louder.

"Mister Mack," said Mister Meaney. "Please, put the gun down."

"What gun?" said Mister Mack. "Have you any wood in here that you want cut?"

"I don't think so," said Mister Meaney.

"Actually," said another voice behind the counter.

They looked, and saw a small man at a big desk, with his hands way up.

"Actually, Mister Meaney," said the man. "You promised me that you'd get someone to cut a few inches off the legs of this desk because I can't reach my mouse without standing up."

Mister Meaney stared at the man.

"Mister O'Dim," he said. "This is hardly the time to—"

But Mister Mack put the saw up to his shoulder.

"No problem," he said.

Some people screamed and one or two fainted but, when the sawdust cleared, they all saw: the desk was exactly three inches closer to the floor. Mister Mack had done a perfect job.

"Impressed?" said Mister Mack.

"Gulp," said Mister Meaney. "Yes."

"My mouse!" said the man at the desk.

His sandwiches were shredded, all over the floor, his shoelaces were singed and smoking, but he didn't seem to mind.

"Come here, ickle mousey!"

Then they heard a loud voice from outside.

"This is the Garda. Put your hands up."

And Mister Mack put the saw on the counter and lifted his hands into the air. It was keep-your-hands-up-in-the-air day, and he didn't want to spoil the fun.

Jimmy and Robbie heard the door behind them open and they felt the air rush past them, followed by two

Guards, and another two Guards. The bank was suddenly full of Guards.

"Excuse me, Sergeant."

"Get off my foot, Sergeant."

"Oh, I beg your pardon, Sergeant."

The big backs of the Guards got in Jimmy's and Robbie's way and they couldn't see Mister Mack. Then, like two big doors, two big Garda backs moved apart and more Guards came toward Robbie and Jimmy, and Mister Mack was in the middle of them, like the figs in one of his fig-rolls.

He smiled at the boys but he looked worried.

"Tell your mammy," he said over the Garda shoulders.

"Tell her what?" said Robbie.

"I'm not sure," said Mister Mack.

The Garda fig-roll was at the door by now.

"Something about me being in trouble," said Mister Mack. "But I don't know why."

He was gone. And most of the Garda backs were gone. Robbie and Jimmy could see the door and, through the door, they could see two huge Guards closing the doors of a big black van.

"What'll we do now?" said Jimmy.

"We'd better tell Mammy," said Robbie.

"OK," said Jimmy.

They saw Mister Mack's face pressed to the glass of the van door. He saw them and smiled as the van moved away slowly.

"But where is she?"

It had been a day full of problems so far, and this was easily the biggest one, so far. The boys' mother was Billie Jean, and they had no idea where she was.

CHAPTER TEN

Meanwhile . . .

Kayla and Victoria were sitting on a wall, eating chocolate things they'd borrowed from the supermarket.

A black Garda van passed.

"Batteries included," said Victoria.

"Who are you!" Kayla shouted. "Who are you!"

Here's what they meant:

"Will you look at the head on that eejit in the back of the Garda van," said Victoria.

"That's no eejit!" Kayla shouted. "That's my dad!"

They jumped off the wall and hopped on to the bike. But before they could cycle after the Garda van, someone pulled Kayla's jumper and someone else pulled Victoria's. The bike went off by itself.

Robbie and Jimmy held Kayla and Victoria up in the air.

"Do you know where Mammy is?" asked Jimmy.

"Who are you!"

"No idea at all?" asked Robbie.

"Who are you!"

"Maybe America!"

"Who are you!"

"Maybe China! We'll never find her."

CHAPTER ELEVEN

Where was their mother?

The answer is easy but not very helpful.

She could have been anywhere.

What? Like a ghost?

No. Nothing like a ghost. Let me explain.

A week after he walked out of the biscuit factory, Mister Mack and Billie Jean Fleetwood-Mack were getting the dinner ready.

Boring.

They were killing a cow in the back garden. There were moos and blood all over the place.

Really?

No. They were in the kitchen. Billie Jean was peeling the spuds.

"Don't!" yelled a spud. "There's a zip at the back!"

But Billie Jean didn't hear him. She was talking to Mister Mack.

"I was thinking," said Billie Jean.

"You want to break another record," said Mister Mack.

"Yes," said Billie Jean.

Billie Jean was an amazing woman. She'd broken all kinds of records. She was the first woman in the world to climb the Spire, in Dublin. She was the fastest person to climb the Eiffel Tower, in Paris. She was the only woman to straighten the Leaning Tower, in Pisa. She'd made and broken all kinds of records. Second woman to cycle up Mount Everest.

Fastest woman to cycle down Mount Everest. First person to drive a tractor through the National Art Gallery. First woman to break into Mountjoy Jail. There were seven pages of the *Guinness Book of World Records* filled with Billie Jean's records, and that was a record too. Billie Jean couldn't go out the door without breaking a record. Fastest woman ever to cut the grass. She couldn't even go to the door without breaking a record.

First woman ever to bring the milk from the step to the kitchen on a skateboard. Records broke whenever she went near them.

And that was the problem.

Billie Jean was tired of breaking the easy records and she'd decided to go for the big one. She told Mister Mack.

Mister Mack looked at Billie Jean. God, he loved her. If his love could have been measured, it would have been a record – the most love ever felt for an Irishwoman. Billie Jean smiled at him, and Mister Mack broke his own record.

"How long will it take?" he asked.

"It's hard to say," she said. "Eight months, maybe."

"That's a long time," said Mister Mack. "You don't have to walk, do you?"

"No," said Billie Jean. "Any way I like, as long as I don't tell anyone."

"Except me," said Mister Mack.

"That's right," said Billie Jean. "That's the rule."

"I hope I don't blab," said Mister Mack.

"I'm sure you won't," said Billie Jean.

"Because if I do, there's no record. Isn't that right?"

"Yes," said Billie Jean. "But you won't."

Hey.

Yes.

What's going on? What's the record they're talking about?

Good question. But I can't answer it yet.

Why not?

I haven't made it up yet.

Really?

No. I have made it up. But I won't tell you yet, because it's more exciting that way.

No, it isn't.

Shut up.

CHAPTER TWELVE

Meanwhile, Mister Mack was in the police station. He was in a cell, and there were two detectives with him. One of the detectives was nice, and the other one wasn't nice at all. (One of them sweated a lot and smoked cigarettes. Can you guess which one? The answer is coming up.)

"Where's your wife, Mack?" said Not-Nice.

"I'm not telling you," said Mister Mack.

"Why not?" said Not-Nice.

"I just won't," said Mister Mack. "I can't."

"Why not?" said Not-Nice.

"Isn't the weather great for this time of year?" said Nice.

"It's a secret," said Mister Mack.

Not-Nice stared at Mister Mack.

"What age are you, Mack?" he said.

"Thirty-seven," said Mister Mack.

"You don't look a day over thirty," said Nice.

"Thank you," said Mister Mack. "I try to look after myself."

"You're looking at ten years behind bars, Mack," said Not-Nice. "How does that sound?"

"Shocking," said Nice. He lit his cigarette and wiped the sweat from his face.

"So," said Not-Nice. "Where's your wife? She could tell us if that gun's really a saw. Where is she?"

"I'm not telling," said Mister Mack.

CHAPTER THIRTEEN

Meanwhile, Billie Jean Fleetwood-Mack looked up at the blue sky.

"Ah," she said. "This is the life."

Billie Jean was on a raft, somewhere on the Pacific Ocean.

Kayla had been kind of right. Billie Jean was in, maybe, America, and in, maybe, China. She was in between them, floating on the ocean.

The sea was calm. The waves were being very nice, lifting the raft and shoving it gently towards –

she hoped – China. Billie Jean had just had her dinner, a tin of beans. She'd enjoyed it, but it had reminded her a lot of the dinner she'd had the day before, and the day before that. Billie Jean had had a tin of beans every day since she'd climbed on to the raft and pushed it away from the California shore, twenty-four days before. She farted a lot but she didn't mind that, because every fart pushed the raft a few inches closer to – she really hoped – China. But beans were beans – they were boring little lads.

Billie Jean looked up at the sky again.

"Ah," she said, again. "This really is the life."

But she didn't think that this was the life at all. In fact, Billie Jean was bored and lonely. The first part of the trip had been great, across the Atlantic: storms and icebergs and other great stuff. Billie Jean had loved it. The raft fell apart, and she put it back together again, just before a shark ate the hammer and most of the nails. The journey across the United States was great, too, except people kept asking where she was going. And she couldn't tell them. It was against the rules.

"Hey! You're Irish. Where are you going?"

Here are some of Billie Jean's answers:

1. "The shops."
2. "My granny's."
3. "Eh."
4. "Mind your own business."

She was happy when she got to California and built a new raft. And now, here she was. Somewhere in—

On.

On the Pacific. Heading very slowly towards – oh God, she hoped – China. The sea was very calm, she hadn't seen a killer whale in ages, the sky was huge and blue.

Boring.

Billie Jean agreed. It *was* boring.

Then she saw something. In the distance. Land. She wasn't sure. She stared and stared. She looked away, and looked. And she saw — mountains.

Billie Jean ate the rest of her beans. Then she looked at the mountains and farted. The mountains got a tiny bit nearer. She farted again. The

mountains seemed nearer again. She farted all day and all night, even in her sleep. She slept and farted right through the next day, and when she woke up, the bottom of the raft was rubbing sand. Billie Jean was only a few feet from the shore.

She stepped out of the raft. The water was warm. It was a long beach and, before her, trees rose up into the mountains. She looked all around her. It was getting dark. She could see no houses, no boats, no one.

Then, something in the distance caught her eye. Further down the beach, a woman climbed out of a raft, walked to the shore, just like Billie Jean had done. Billie Jean ran to meet her.

"Hi," said Billie Jean.

"Hi," said the woman.

"Where are we?" asked Billie Jean.

"I'm not sure," said the woman. "Maybe China."

They suddenly looked at each other, very carefully. They were both Irish, and very far from home. They were both dressed for travel and adventure. They both looked like women who ran into strong wind and jumped off high things. They both farted at the exact same time, and they knew: they were both going after the same record – first woman to go around the world without telling anyone.

Hang on. She told Mister Mack.

You're allowed to tell just one person before you start.

That's stupid.

No, it isn't. If you tell one person, it proves that you really went off to break the record and that it wasn't just an accident or a coincidence.

The two women looked at each other.

"Seeyeh," said Billie Jean.

She started running.

CHAPTER FOURTEEN

Meanwhile, the Mack kids and Victoria were at home in the kitchen, eating their breakfast: maple syrup straight out of the bottle. It was the morning after Mister Mack had been arrested. The kids had all slept together in their parents' big bed.

Boring.

I agree. The kids were having a meeting.

"How do you know Mammy's going around the world?" asked Jimmy.

"Who are you."

"You were under the table when she told Dad?"

Kayla nodded.

"Why do you think she's in China?" asked Robbie.

Kayla shrugged.

"Who are you."

"Because she left a month ago, and that's how long it would take you to get to China if you went west, across the Atlantic Ocean, the United States and the Pacific?"

Kayla nodded.

"We'll need Rover," said Jimmy.

Kayla nodded. And so did Victoria.

They were ready to go.

CHAPTER FIFTEEN

But Rover wasn't.

"China?" he said. "You're jesting."

They were in Rover's shed. Rover was lying on his rug, reading the greyhound racing results.

To adults, Rover was the standard dog. He barked, he pooed, he sometimes growled. He scratched on the door when he wanted to get out, and he whined when he wanted to come back in. He did clever things too. He went to the shop and brought home his owner's newspaper, in his mouth. But what his owner didn't know was, Rover always stopped and read the paper on the way home. His owner often looked at his phone bill and gasped.

"Janey, Rover," he'd say. "I don't remember making all those calls."

He didn't make the calls. Rover did.

"Woof," Rover would say, and wag his tail.

While his owner slept or went to work, Rover ran several successful businesses. He supplied poo to the Gigglers, who made grown-ups who'd been mean to children stand on it. He ran a dog talent agency. All those dogs you see on the telly,

Rover supplied them all. All those dogs who do funny, cute things in the home video programmes – they were all Rover's. They hated the work.

"It's so humiliating, darling."

But the money was good, and ten per cent of it was Rover's. The puppy that runs through the house in the toilet paper ad – he was a Rover client. That dog in the Bus Eireann ad, the red setter that runs beside the bus – he was another one of Rover's.

INTERESTING INFORMATION:

"Bus Eireann" means "Irish Bus". It's a bus company. The funny thing is, though, the red setter in the Bus Eireann ad isn't Irish at all. His name is Tibor, and he comes from Hungary. Back to Rover and the story.

And that wasn't all. Hey, adult, if you're reading this book with a kid: did you ever answer your phone and hear a voice:

"Good morning. Do you mind if I ask you some questions? It will only take ten minutes of your time."

That was probably Rover you were talking to.

"Are you happy with your bank?"

Probably Rover.

"Have you thought about insurance?"

Probably Rover.

"How's it going, pal. Would you be interested in a leather jacket?"

Definitely Rover.

Rover could sell anything. He even sold Germany once, over the phone, to a man in Ringsend.

"D'you want it delivered, or will you collect?"

"Delivered," said the man.

"No problem," said Rover. "And I'll tell you what. We'll throw in Austria for an extra ten euro. How does that sound?"

"Lovely."

But that was years ago. Rover was older now, and taking it easy.

"China?" he said. "You're jesting."

He waited for them to go.

"Ah, come on, Rover."

"You can do it."

"Who are you?"

"Please, Rover."

"Batteries included."

Rover looked at them over his reading glasses.

"Get lost," he said. "I've retired."

"What age are you?" asked Jimmy.

"Ten," said Rover.

"That's not old enough to retire," said Robbie.

"I'm seventy if you convert it into dog years," said Rover.

"That's not that old," said Robbie.

"Eighty-nine if you convert it into euros," said Rover.

"That's still not that old," said Robbie. "Our granny's ninety, and she plays for Shamrock Rovers."

"I've seen her play," said Rover. "Believe me, she's old."

He got back to the racing results.

"So, you won't help us find our mammy?" asked Robbie.

Rover didn't answer.

"So, you'll let the orphan catcher take us away and throw us into an orphanage?" asked Jimmy.

Then Kayla said something in a tiny, tearful voice. And she held out her little hands.

"Who are you?"

Rover stood up.

"OK, OK. You win."

Here is what Kayla actually said:

"Please, sir, can I have some more?"

INTERESTING INFORMATION:

Kayla was a brilliant impressionist. She had just done her Oliver Twist impression for Rover. She could also do impressions of the following people: Eminem, Beyoncé, Nelson Mandela, the Hulk and Scooby-Doo.

"OK, OK," said Rover. "You win. When do we start?"

"Batteries included!"

And Victoria and Kayla jumped on to his back.

"Now?" said Rover. "Well, I'll have to go to the toilet first. The ol' bladder isn't what it used to be. Get off me."

"Who are you?"

"No, I can't go while I'm running. Get off."

CHAPTER SIXTEEN

Meanwhile, Billie Jean was running around Beijing, the biggest city in China — the first woman ever to bypass Beijing. She had planned on walking into Beijing and staying a few days. But, now, she couldn't do that.

She looked over her shoulder.

The other woman was still there, right behind her, the exact same distance.

Billie Jean kept running.

THE DAILY OUTRAGE

BANK ROBBER HAS TERRIFIED
NEIGHBOURS FOR YEARS,
by Our Staff Reporter, Paddy Hackery.

Crazed bank robber Mister Mack is a dangerous man, according to his neighbours.

"I saw him cough once," said a woman who did not want to be named. "And he didn't even put his hand to his mouth. He nearly killed the lot of us."

Every house has a story to tell.

"He once shouted 'Nice day' at me, and it wasn't a nice day at all. It was horrible."

"He once helped me across the street," said an elderly neighbour. "And I didn't want to cross the street. I was stuck on the wrong side for four days, all because of him."

"He's a bit of a weirdo," said a local shopkeeper. "He doesn't even have a first name."

Mister Mack looked up from the newspaper.

"I do so have a first name," he said. "It's Mister."

THE STORY OF HOW MISTER MACK GOT HIS FIRST NAME

Jimmy and Robbie's teacher was called Mister Eejit. He got that name when a man came cycling down the street checking all the names of the people who lived in the different houses. Mister Eejit's father was building the house, and he was holding a concrete block when the man got off his bike. "What is your name?" said the man at the exact same time that Mister Eejit's father let the block slip out of his fingers. The block smashed his toes as the man said "name" and Mister Eejit's father yelled, "Eejit!" giving out to himself for dropping the block. By the time Mister Eejit's father had nursed and kissed his poor tootsies, the man was cycling away. "My name's O'Malley!" he shouted. But it was too late. His name was now Eejit, and so was his son's, Robbie and Jimmy's teacher.

Meanwhile, the man cycled around the corner and stopped at the next house. Mister Mack's mother and father lived there. The man got off his bike and rang the bell. Mister Mack's father opened the door. He looked very happy and tired. "What is your name?" said the man. "Anthony Mack," said Mister Mack's father. "And does anyone else live here?" said the man. "Yes," said Mister Mack's father. "Name?" said the man. "Mary Margaret Mooney-Mack," said Mister Mack's father. "Any children?" asked the man. And this was why Mister Mack's father looked so happy and tired. Mister Mack had been born the night before. Mister Mack's father had just come home from the hospital. "Oh, yes," he said proudly. "A boy." "Name?" said the man. And here was the problem. Mister Mack's parents hadn't thought of a name yet. Mister Mack's father looked at the man. "Well," he said. "I don't know, eh, Mister, eh. . ." "Mister," said the man, and he wrote it down. He got back on his bike. "A strange name," he said. "But we live in very strange times." "But," said Mister Mack's father. But it was too late. The man had cycled away. Mister Mack's father met his new neighbour at the gate. "My son's name is Mister," he said. "That's nothing," said his neighbour. "My son's name is Eejit." And that's a true story.

Mister Mack threw the newspaper on to the floor of his cell. He didn't want to read it any more.

The door opened, and the two detectives walked in.

"Good morning, Mister Mack," said Nice. "Have you had your breakfast?"

"Tell us about the gun, Mack," said Not-Nice.

"No," said Mister Mack.

"No, you won't tell us about the gun?"

"No, I haven't had my breakfast. And it isn't a gun. It's a saw."

"Here we go again," said Not-Nice. "What did you saw with it, Mack?"

"What would you like, Mister Mack?" said Nice.

"Wood," said Mister Mack.

"For your breakfast?" said Nice.

"No," said Mister Mack. "It's what the saw was for. Cutting wood."

"Of course it was," said Nice. "Cornflakes?"

"I'm confused," said Mister Mack.

"You're guilty," said Not-Nice.

"Ah, leave the poor man alone," said Nice. "He hasn't had his breakfast yet."

"So, where's the famous Billie Jean, Mack?" said Not-Nice. "Why isn't she here to rescue you?"

Mister Mack closed his eyes.

PROBABLY CHAPTER SEVENTEEN

Meanwhile, Rover was ready to go.

"What kept you?" said Robbie. "You were in the toilet all night."

"You'll understand when you're older, pal," said Rover. "Are we ready?"

Kayla and Victoria jumped onto his back.

Here was the plan. Kayla, Victoria and Rover would run around the world and find Billie Jean.

"No sweat," said Rover.

Meanwhile, Robbie and Jimmy would stay in Dublin.

"Nice one," said Rover.

But they weren't going to hang around, waiting for a happy ending. They were going to dig a tunnel under the Garda station and rescue Mister Mack.

"I'm good at tunnels," said Rover. "They're my speciality."

"No," said Jimmy. "You find our mammy."

"Fair enough," said Rover.

"Who are you?" asked Kayla.

"The M50," said Rover. "The traffic shouldn't be too bad."

And they were gone. Just like that, they were out of Rover's garden, and Jimmy and Robbie were alone.

"Let's get the shovels," said Jimmy.

"OK," said Robbie. "But will we watch a bit a telly first?"

"OK," said Jimmy.

They went into their house.

DEFINITELY CHAPTER EIGHTEEN

Meanwhile, Billie Jean was running along the Great Wall of China.

Billie Jean looked behind. The other woman had caught up with her. Billie Jean tripped. She fell and landed on one of her knees.

"Ouch."

She looked, and saw the other woman run ahead. The woman turned as she ran.

"I'm sorry that happened," she shouted. "Do you want me to stop?"

Billie Jean waved.

"No," she shouted back. "I'll catch up with you."

"Oh no, you won't."

"We'll see about that," said Billie Jean quietly.

She took off her rucksack and opened it. She had some special medicines in the bag, and one of them was called Mendo-nee.

"I hope this stuff works," she said.

Meanwhile, Missis Meaney, the orphan catcher, was looking for the Mack kids. She was walking down their street, getting closer to the house. She was a nasty woman. She had a mole on her chin, and her clothes were too tight. Her shoes were loud, and she had a nasty laugh. She had a big net, a bigger bum, and a bad, bad temper. (Sinister fact: She was the bank manager's sister, and he had told her that the Mack children were at home, all alone, without their parents.) She kicked the door open.

"Ha ha," she shouted. "Caught you!" The family looked up from their breakfast.

"Wrong house, missis," said the father.

"Oh," she said.

"And you'll have to pay for that lock."

"Oh."

She tried hard to look nasty again. She sniffed the air.

"I smell orphans," she said.

"No, missis," said the father. "That's the toast. I burned it."

His children, all ten of them, laughed. The orphan catcher hated that sound. She ran out of the house. She was blushing and furious. She sniffed again.

"I'll show them," she said. "I *do* smell orphans."

She headed for the Mack house.

Meanwhile, the M50, the motorway that goes around Dublin, was blocked.

"Did you ever see anything like this traffic?" said Rover.

Meanwhile, the orphan catcher charged into the Mack house.

"Ha ha! Caught you!"

But no one was there. The house seemed empty. She heard voices and crept to the sitting room.

"They're watching telly," she said. "The lazy little messers."

She pushed the door.

"Ha ha."

But the room was empty. The telly was on, but no one was there. There was a film on, *The Great Escape*. She watched men digging a tunnel. Then the actor Steve McQueen came onto the screen. He was in a cell, throwing a baseball at the wall.

"Oh, I like him," she said, and she sat down to watch.

Meanwhile, Jimmy and Robbie were under the telly, digging a tunnel.

"I wonder what's on telly?" said Jimmy.

"Probably something boring," said Robbie.

Meanwhile, Mister Mack was alone in his cell. He was sitting on the floor, leaning against the wall.

"God, this is boring," he said. "I wish I had a baseball, like that fella in *The Great Escape*."

Then he saw something. A match. On the floor. The nice detective had dropped it. Mister Mack picked it up.

Meanwhile, Rover had kidnapped a motorbike. With Kayla behind him and Victoria on the handlebars, he drove through the traffic, and over it. Drivers screamed and fainted when they heard the noise on their roofs.

"What do you think you're doing?" a driver yelled.

"Looking for this kid's ma," said Rover. "Have a nice day."

They had just reached the Tallaght roundabout.

Back to the story.

The cars and trucks in front of Rover went around the roundabout. But Rover drove straight on to it.

Was he taking a shortcut?

Yes, he was. But he didn't just drive across the grass, to get to the other side. In fact, he didn't drive across the roundabout at all. He drove into it. He disappeared. The bike, Kayla, Victoria, Rover – they all disappeared.

Rover knew all the world's short-cuts. He knew the little ones, like the quickest way from your house to the shop. And the bigger ones, like the quickest way to get from Dublin to Donegal. (HINT: Don't go through Argentina.) But that wasn't all. Rover knew all the secret shortcuts in the world. He knew a wardrobe in London that brought you straight to Narnia. He knew a secret railway platform in Euston Station, in London, that brought you straight to the Watermill, a pub in Raheny. And he knew a hole behind a bush in the middle of the Tallaght roundabout that brought you straight to –

"Who are you!"

"That's right, kid," said Rover. "Las Vegas."

He climbed off the motorbike. And,

for the first time that day, the motorbike spoke.

"Coo-il," he said. "Where's Elvis?"

And he drove off, into the lights and noise.

Meanwhile, Robbie and Jimmy were making progress. They'd tunnelled under ten houses, and across the street. But they were running out of wood to support the roof and stop the tunnel from caving in. So far, they'd used their bunk beds and the stairs to the attic. And they had to get rid of some of the muck before they could dig any further.

They crawled back under the sitting room. They could hear the telly.

"Crazed gunman, Mister Mack, remains in custody today. More in our news bulletin, after the movie."

Robbie climbed up, and out the back of the telly. There was no one in the sitting room. He whispered down to Jimmy.

"All clear."

Jimmy handed buckets of muck up to Robbie, and he emptied them out the window, into the garden.

Meanwhile, the orphan catcher was in the kitchen. She was making a jam-and-cornflake sandwich.

"War films always make me hungry," she said.

She stopped. She thought she'd heard something. She sniffed.

"Orphans," she said.

She picked up her net. She crept slowly to the sitting-room door. She jumped in.

"Ha ha!"

It was empty.

Meanwhile, Robbie had climbed out the sitting-room window and gone around to the kitchen door. He was hungry. He opened the door and saw the sandwich on the table.

Meanwhile, Jimmy was in the sitting room, inside the telly, looking out at the orphan catcher.

Meanwhile, Mister Mack had started to scrape the cement between the bricks of the cell wall, with the match.

The cement crumbled, and dust fell to the floor.

Meanwhile, Robbie picked up the sandwich and walked into the hall. He took a bite – yeuk – and came to the sitting room door.

"A warning to all kids!"

He saw Jimmy's face, pressed to the inside of the screen.

"Kids with sandwiches should never walk into sitting rooms!"

Robbie stopped.

"A government report just released advises all children to stay out of sitting rooms if they have sandwiches."

Robbie heard a voice.

"What's that rubbish?"

He heard a big bum slap down on the couch. He saw a big arm, and a hand holding the remote control, pointing at the telly. He saw Jimmy's face disappear.

Meanwhile, more cement fell to the

cell floor, and on to Mister Mack's bare feet.

Meanwhile, the orphan catcher went back into the kitchen. Her sandwich was there, where she'd left it. But there was a bite taken out of it. And there was something else, a piece of paper, beside the plate. She picked it up and read: "You make brutal sandwiches – ha ha. Signed: The Phantom Orphan."

Meanwhile, Robbie was back in the tunnel, with Jimmy. He'd climbed in the sitting-room window when the orphan catcher went back to the kitchen. They were digging really fast now, getting nearer and nearer to the Garda station.

Meanwhile, Billie Jean was catching up with the other woman. They had galloped into Mongolia and they were now halfway across the Gobi Desert.

"It's lovely, isn't it?" the other woman shouted back to Billie Jean.

"Gorgeous," Billie Jean shouted back.

Meanwhile, Rover and the girls were charging across the Mojave Desert. The sand and stones were hot, so Rover had to go dead fast so his feet wouldn't burn too badly.

"Ouch, ouch, ouch, ouch, ouch!"

Meanwhile, the writer decided to make a cup of coffee. He stood up and walked to his office door.

"Hey!" Rover shouted. "Come back here!"

The writer went back to his computer. He sat down and wrote this: Meanwhile, Rover and the kids had run across the Mojave Desert and were now running along a beach near Los Angeles.

"That's better," said Rover.

The weather was great, but not too hot. It was perfect hairy-dog weather. A nice breeze lifted the hair from Rover's eyes and made him look even more handsome and intelligent than usual. As he ran along the edge of the water of Rocka-Hound Beach, the only beach in the world specially for dogs—

"Good man," said Rover. "Keep going."

As Rover ran along the beach, through the breakwater, the canine beach-babes and beach-bums stepped back to admire him.

"Wow," they said. "Awesome."

Meanwhile, the writer got up from

his desk to make a cup of coffee.

"Fire away," said Rover as he galloped elegantly through the surf.

"Who are you?" asked Kayla.

"Shut up, you," said Rover. "I'm not showing off."

The writer went into the kitchen and filled the kettle with cold water. He brought the kettle over to the counter and plugged it in. While he waited for the kettle to boil, he wiped the counter with a damp cloth and—

Boring.

The kettle exploded, and the writer was thrown across the kitchen. He hit the door, and it smashed as he went through it. He landed in the garden. He lay there, unconscious, for three hours.

Meanwhile, Robbie and Jimmy kept digging but were making no progress. They didn't move forward and the bucket didn't fill, even though they kept throwing muck into it. And Billie

Jean noticed something. She was running faster than she'd ever run before, but the mountains in front were getting no nearer. Mister Mack noticed something too. The air around his face was full of cement dust and little brick bits, floating, not dropping. And Rover noticed something. The beach went on for ever – it seemed like that. Every time he looked, he saw the same dogs looking at him.

"Wow."

"Awesome."

"Wow."

"Awesome."

"Wow."

"Awesome."

He looked down at his paws. They were moving, but he wasn't going anywhere.

Meanwhile, the writer was still lying in the garden, still unconscious. It had started to rain.

"Hey, pal."

It was Rover. But the writer couldn't hear him because he was seriously injured and fighting for his life.

"Hey, pal. Wake up."

The rain continued to fall, but the writer couldn't feel it.

"Wake up!"

"I'm unconscious, Rover," said the writer.

"If you don't wake up quick, I'll go over there and bite the leg off you."

Suddenly, the writer woke up. He jumped to his feet.

"That was close," he said.

"Hurry up!"

The writer bravely ignored his aches and pains and ran back into the house. He decided not to bother with coffee—

"Wise move."

And he ran straight back to his office and jumped on to his swivel chair. A pain shot through his body, but he ignored it. Blood ran from his forehead, over his eyes, but he wiped it away with his sleeve. He looked at the screen. He rubbed his hands together, then started writing.

"Wow!"

"Awesome!"

Rover felt the ground under his feet again. He felt the water, and the wind in his fur. He was moving again, racing along the beach. The canine beach-babes swooned.

"Seeyis, girls," said Rover. "Duty calls."

And he was gone, galloping across the sands of Southern California.

"See this rabbit hole in front of us?" he said.

"Batteries included," said Victoria.

"Gopher hole, rabbit hole," said Rover. "I don't care what kind of a hole it is, as long as we fit. Next stop, Beijing!"

And Rover dived down the hole.

CHAPTER . . . WHAT CHAPTER IS IT?

The writer went back to check.

CHAPTER NINETEEN

It was later in the day, and Mister Mack was worried. He'd made a hole in the cell wall. It was only a small hole, but the not-nice detective was leaning right beside it.

"Well," said Not-Nice. "What have you been up to?"

Mister Mack gulped.

"Nothing much," he said.

"Been trying to escape?" said Not-Nice.

"Not really," said Mister Mack.

"Nobody ever escaped from this station," said Nice. "Do you know why?"

"Why?" said Mister Mack.

"It's brand-new," said Nice. "It only opened on Monday."

"Is that right?"

"That's right."

"Enough small talk," said Not-Nice.

He stepped away from the wall and sat in front of Mister Mack.

"What were you going to do with the money?"

"What money?" said Mister Mack.

"Come on. The money you were going to take from the bank."

"I wasn't going to take any. . ."

Those dots are there because Mister Mack didn't finish what he was going to say, because Not-Nice threw a newspaper on to the desk.

"You were going to run off and join your wife, wherever she's hiding. Weren't you?"

Mister Mack looked at the paper.

THE EVENING INSULT

WIFE OF BANK ROBBER GOES INTO HIDING

by Our Special Reporter, Mary O'Contrary

SHE'S EVEN SCARIER THAN HIM, SAY NEIGHBOURS

Billie Jean Fleetwood-Mack, wife of crazed bank robber Mister Mack, has gone into hiding, according to their neighbours.

"They were in it together," said a woman who did not want to be named. "She had all the latest gear. Trainers, tracksuits, crash helmets. The money had to come from somewhere."

"I saw her in the supermarket once," said another neighbour. "And she had enough food in her trolley to feed a family of five for three or four days. I always wondered where they got the money."

Ms Fleetwood-Mack has been terrifying the neighbours for years.

"She dived off her roof once and landed in our wheely bin," said an elderly neighbour.

"I haven't been the same since. It's been much nicer here since she went on the run." But where is the record-breaking Ms Fleetwood-Mack?

"The attic," one neighbour suggested. "She was always up there."

"Somewhere sunny," said another. "That's where I'd go if I was a bank robber's molly."

READERS' POLL: Where do YOU think she is? Have YOUR say.

Mister Mack looked up from the newspaper.

"That's just silly," he said.

"Oh yeah?" said Not-Nice.

"Yeah."

"How silly?"

Mister Mack stuck out his tongue and crossed his eyes.

"That silly," he said.

"You're beginning to get on my nerves," said Not-Nice. "Where is she?"

"I don't. . ."

Those dots are there because Mister Mack didn't finish what he was going to say, because he'd been distracted. The nice detective had walked over to the wall and, now, he put his finger in the hole.

"Will you look at that," said Nice. "It's a disgrace, so it is. A brand-new wall with a hole like that."

He took a handkerchief out of his pocket and stuffed it into the hole.

"You'll catch your death with the draught coming through that hole," he said. "We'll have to get it fixed."

Mister Mack moaned. He'd spent hours making that hole.

"Why did you moan?" asked Not-Nice.

"No reason," said Mister Mack.

"Why?" said Not-Nice.

And Mister Mack decided to really annoy Not-Nice.

"That's for me to know and you to find out," he said.

"Aagh," said Not-Nice.

He walked out of the cell and slammed the door.

CHAPTER TWENTY

This Chapter Is Sponsored by Happy-Dig, Makers of the World's Best Shovels and Spades

Meanwhile, Robbie and Jimmy stopped digging. They'd just heard something, above them.

"That was a door," said Robbie.

"Yeah," said Jimmy.

"Dad," said Robbie.

And Jimmy nodded. The boys had grown up listening to doors slamming just like that one. It was a Mister Mack kind of slam.

But Mister Mack didn't slam the door. That's true. But a Mister Mack slam was never the sound of a door being slammed by Mister Mack. A Mister Mack slam was the sound of a door being slammed by someone who had just been talking to Mister Mack. The boys knew the sound well, and they loved it. When they were much younger, playing with their toys on the floor, they'd hear a door slam and they'd look at each other.

"Da da?" one of them would say.

"Da da," the other would answer.

Mister Mack was a nice man, but something about him made people slam doors.

"Will we go to the pictures?" said Billie Jean, once.

"I'm sorting out my socks," said Mister Mack.

"But the film starts in ten minutes.

Can the socks not wait?"

Mister Mack picked up some of the odd socks.

"But the poor things are lonely," he said. "And I saw the film this afternoon. She runs off with the doctor, and the car chase isn't very good."

Slam!

He looked up. Billie Jean was gone, and the bedroom door was wobbling.

"Mister Mack?"

It was Mister Mack's boss in the biscuit factory.

"Yes?" said Mister Mack.

"Have you a minute?"

Mister Mack searched his pockets. He found two euro, a banana, his keys and one of Kayla's baby teeth.

"No," he said. "I don't have a minute. Sorry."

Slam!

Mother Teresa, of Calcutta, the most famous nun in the world, once called at the Mack house. Mister

Mack answered the door.

"Hello," he said. "You look familiar."

"Would you please give some money for the poor?" asked Mother Teresa.

"How do I know you won't waste it on drugs?" said Mister Mack.

Slam!

Mother Teresa was so angry, she beat up three teenagers and threw her mobile phone through the pet shop window.

"Tweet tweet!" said a budgie. "Is that who I think it is?"

"She must have met Mister – tweet tweet – Mack."

It got to the point where Mister Mack didn't even have to speak. He got that look on his face, and people slammed the door. Billie Jean slammed a door before she spoke to him, even if she was speaking to him on the phone.

"Abah, abah."

It was Kayla's idea. And it worked. Once she'd slammed the door, Billie Jean didn't mind what silly thing Mister Mack said or did. It became a joke. And he invented a special door for Billie Jean, for her birthday. It was on wheels so she could pull it wherever she went and always have a door to slam if she wasn't near a real one.

Anyway, it was a Mister Mack slam that the boys had just heard. Right over their heads.

They could see each other grinning in the dark.

CHAPTER TWENTY-ONE

Meanwhile, Billie Jean was running through Omsk, a city in Russia. The traffic was mad because people were going home from work. Drivers were honking and shrieking, and their cars were making a lot of noise too. But as Billie Jean ran past a block of flats, she heard a door slam.

"Oh dear," she said. "How I miss Mister Mack."

And she cried a little bit as she finally caught up with the other woman.

"Will we finish together?" said the other woman. "Side by side."

"We will not," said Billie Jean. "None of that women-together nonsense for me. I'm going to win."

And she ran ahead of the other woman.

"Cheerio."

CHAPTER TWENTY-TWO

This Chapter Is Sponsored by
Bow-Wow-Spex,
Makers of Quality Glasses
and Contact Lenses
for Your Dog

"Next stop, Beijing."

The last time we saw Rover and the girls, they had just jumped down a rabbit hole that had been made by a very big gopher. Now, the street light came charging in at them. Rover

369

jumped out of the tunnel.

"Hello, Beijing!"

And there, in front of them, was the Spire. Rover put on his glasses.

"It looks like the one in Dublin," he said.

He looked at the people passing.

"And they don't look very Chinese."

"Who are you?" said Kayla.

"Who are you calling an eejit?" said Rover.

But he had to admit it. They were back in Dublin, on O'Connell Street, thousands of miles from where he'd expected them to be.

"Excellent," said Rover. "It's all going to plan. Come on."

He started running.

But he only ran ten yards, and stopped.

"It's no good, girls," said Rover. "Poor ol' Rover's flummoxed. What'll we do?"

CHAPTER TWENTY-THREE

This Chapter Is Sponsored by
Keep-'Em-In,
Makers of Secure Prisons
and Play-Schools

Mister Mack sat in his cell. The slam was the only other thing in the cell, and it was dying.

Poor Mister Mack. Tomorrow morning they'd be coming to take him to court. And, after that, he'd be all alone for years. In a cell. In a prison. He knew Billie Jean could have saved him. But she was thousands of miles away. A tear crawled out of his eye and rolled down his cheek. He was so unhappy.

How unhappy?

Do you have a dog?

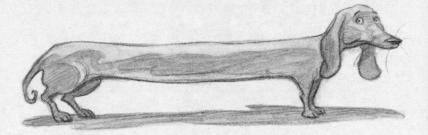

Yeah.

What's its name?

Noodles.

Well, Noodles died this morning.

Oh no!

Are you unhappy?

Yeah.

Well, Mister Mack was even unhappier. The tear rolled down his cheek and—

I want Noodles.

I'll tell you what. If you promise not to interrupt again, Noodles might just come back to life.

Really?

Promise?

Promise.

Noodles isn't dead. He's just asleep. But Mister Mack was awake and very unhappy. The tear rolled down his cheek.

Then he heard something. A knock on the floor.

Meanwhile, Kayla and Victoria explained the plan to Rover.

"Who are you?"

"Batteries included."

"Who are YOU?"

"Batteries included and included and included and batteries!"

"Fair enough," said Rover.

"Included!"

What does all that mean?

Meanwhile, a little dog called Noodles ran out into the middle of O'Connell Street, right in front of a bus and—

Sorry, sorry, I forgot.

Luckily, the bus wasn't moving. Noodles jumped back on to the path. He passed a dog called Rover.

"How's it going, Rover?"

"Not too bad, Noodles."

"So," said Rover. "Where now?"

"Who are you."

"The airport!? But I know a shortcut."

"Who *are* you."

"OK, OK. The airport."

And Rover ran up Dorset Street.

Here was Kayla and Victoria's plan. Instead of chasing after Billie Jean, they'd go in the other direction and catch her coming the other way. Billie Jean had left Ireland and travelled west, across the Atlantic Ocean and America. Rover and the girls had tried to catch up with her. But now, they'd go in the opposite direction, east. With a bit of luck, they'd meet her on her way back, because the world is round. And if you go one way, you'll always come back the other way, even if it feels like you're still going the same way.

Meanwhile, Mister Mack watched the tear that had rolled down his cheek. He'd just heard something. A knock on the floor. The tear hit the floor and bounced right back up into his eye. The eye was surprised, and so was Mister Mack. And the knocking continued. Mister Mack put his ear to the floor. He heard a soft knock.

He moved his ear, and the knocking was louder. He moved again – louder. Again – very loud. Again, and the floor whacked his ear.

"Ouch," said Mister Mack.

"Dad?" said the floor.

Meanwhile, a plane called EI 787 was about to take off, going to Frankfurt, a city in Germany.

"That's a lovely starry sky up there," said EI 787, to himself. "Oh oh, here's the end of the runway. I'd better get up. One. Two – ah!"

EI 787 had just felt Rover's teeth.

As the wheels left the ground, Rover jumped and bit one of them. And he hung on, as EI 787 flew over Dublin Bay, higher and higher, and then Victoria and Kayla scrambled off Rover's back. They climbed to the top of the big wheel. They had a great view from up there – the necklace of lights around the bay, Bull Island, the mountains.

"Who are you!"

Kayla pointed.

"That's right, kid," said Rover as he climbed up beside them. "That's the poo I did this morning. I'm not sure why, but I am kind of proud of it."

They could see it under a streetlight.

"Batteries included."

"Thanks," said Rover. "The Gigglers will love that one."

The wheel started moving, rising slowly into the plane.

"Hang on," said Rover.

They saw no more of Dublin as they were lifted into EI 787.

"It's going to be cold," said Rover. "Really, really freezing."

Kayla and Victoria pulled up their hoods.

"That's grand," said Rover.

Meanwhile, Mister Mack said nothing. He'd never spoken to a floor before, but then, a floor had never called him Dad before. He stopped looking at the floor.

But it did it again.

"Dad?"

Mister Mack looked at the walls and the ceiling.

"Dad?!"

He looked at the door.

"Dad??!!!"

He gave up.

"I'm sorry," he said. "But I'm not your dad."

"Dad!!!??? It's Jimmy!"

"Jimmy?"

"Dad?"

"Is that you, Jimmy?"

"Yes."

"Dad!"

"And Robbie?"

"Hi."

And Mister Mack knew.

"You've come to rescue me."

The tear that had jumped back into his eye climbed back out again.

Meanwhile, Billie Jean had crossed

the border into Poland. She was happy, and feeling happier with every step. She was nearly home. Just Poland, Germany, Holland, a quick swim across the North Sea, across England, another swim, and she'd be there. Back home to her family. She was dying to see them again, to hug and cuddle them. And she'd be the winner, the first woman ever to go around the world without telling anyone.

She ran through miles and miles of wheat. Wheat, wheat and more of it, swaying in the gentle evening breeze.

But the breeze was suddenly stronger, and the other woman flew past Billie Jean. Billie Jean tried to keep up.

"How come you can suddenly run so fast?" she shouted.

"I'm allergic to wheat," the woman shouted back. "Ha ha."

I wish I was, thought Billie Jean as she watched the other woman disappear into the dust and the darkness.

But Billie Jean was allergic to only one thing: Irish music. But there was no Irish music in Poland, so she couldn't keep up with the woman. She couldn't even see her any more.

Meanwhile, the orphan catcher – remember her? – was trying to fix the telly.

"Where's Steve McQueen?" she asked.

She looked behind the telly and saw the hole.

"Ha ha," she said. "Just as I thought."

She started to climb down.

Meanwhile, Mister Mack was scraping the cement between the floor tiles with his fingernail. He could hear the boys below him scraping too.

"Is Kayla with you?" he asked.

"No," said Jimmy. "She's gone looking for Mammy."

"Oh fine," said Mister Mack. "Just as long as she's not in any trouble."

Meanwhile, Kayla was dangling from the wheel as EI 787 prepared to land at Frankfurt Airport. Victoria was beside her. Rover was upside down, clinging to the wheel.

They'd been busy during the flight. They'd opened most of the suitcases in the plane, looking for clothes that would make good parachutes. As the wheels were lowered, all the clothes from the suitcases poured out of the plane. Trousers, shirts, socks, knickers, shoes. They all fell out of EI 787 and dropped slowly through the night to the ground.

"Right," said Rover. "I'm getting bored up here. Let's get going."

Kayla and Victoria slid down the wheel – the plane was 10,000 feet above the ground – and grabbed Rover's fur.

"That's right," said Rover. "Give us a scratch while you're at it."

They held on to Rover's back.

"Ready?" said Rover.

"Who are you?"

And Rover jumped.

Meanwhile, Billie Jean had run across the border into Germany. But she couldn't see the other woman. There was no wheat now, but the woman must have been miles ahead.

"I'll never catch her," said Billie Jean.

She was beginning to feel very tired.

Meanwhile, the orphan catcher was crawling through the tunnel. She stopped, and sniffed.

"I can smell them," she said. "The little orphans."

Meanwhile, Mister Mack's fingernail felt something. Another fingernail. And soon the cement began to drop away and Mister Mack could see his children's fingers.

Under the tile, Robbie and Jimmy got ready and pushed the tile. The first thing they saw was Mister Mack's nose.

"Hi, Dad."

"Hi, boys," said the nose.

Meanwhile, Rover was falling to Germany. He was surrounded by shirts and blouses, vests and bras and waistcoats. Kayla and Victoria had rucksacks on their backs.

"OK," said Rover. "Fire away."

Kayla opened the zip of her rucksack, and a big beautiful dress flew out and filled up with air.

"Batteries included!"

At the same time, Victoria did the

same thing. Her dress filled with air, and the two little girls shot back up. Rover went with them, because they were holding tight to his fur. They shot right past EI 787's nose.

"There go two girls on a dog," said the pilot.

"Yeah yeah yeah," said the co-pilot. "The sky is full of them at this time of night."

Meanwhile, the boys climbed up into Mister Mack's cell.

And meanwhile, the orphan catcher was getting closer and closer.

And meanwhile, a German boy called Klaus was in trouble. He was late for his dinner and he'd lost one of his shoes. He knew his mother would be annoyed. He was always losing his shoes. He was walking home now, very slowly. This is what he sounded like: stomp, slap, stomp, slap, stomp, slap. Suddenly, a shoe hit him on the head. It had fallen 10,000 feet, so it hurt.

But before he realized that he was in great pain, he saw that the shoe was the  exact same as the one he'd lost. The pain ran away, and Klaus looked up. He saw a dog and two girls sailing over his head. *"Danke,"* he shouted.

"No problem, *mein Herr,"* the dog shouted back.

Meanwhile, a very fast woman ran past Klaus. And Rover saw her.

"There's a fast woman down there, look. God, she's a flyer. She must be Irish."

The girls looked, but it wasn't Billie Jean.

"Keep your eyes peeled," said Rover.

Meanwhile, Mister Mack hugged the boys.

"Let's go," said Robbie.

"Where?" said Mister Mack.

"Back down," said Jimmy. "Out of here. Home."

"Ah yes," said Mister Mack. "But, you know, I was making a hole in the wall over there. It seems a shame to waste it."

"Come on, Dad," said Robbie.

He knew how to move his father.

"There are fig-rolls in the kitchen."

And Mister Mack jumped into the hole.

Meanwhile, Billie Jean was running across a bridge. The bridge crossed the River Main, but Billie Jean didn't notice the river or the lights that shone on the water. There were two reasons for this: she was very tired. And Rover landed on her.

Billie Jean and Rover spun in the air, and this was lucky for Billie Jean

because she landed on Rover. The two dresses landed on her, followed by the two girls. Rover decided that the time had come to break his rule about talking in front of adults.

"Get off," he said.

Billie Jean pulled the dresses off her head.

"Who are you?" said Kayla.

"Kayla!" said Billie Jean.

"Batteries included!"

"And Victoria!" said Billie Jean. "What are you doing here? You must tell me everything."

"I said get off," said Rover.

Billie Jean looked down and saw that she was sitting on fur.

"Hurry up!"

Talking fur.

She jumped off Rover, and Rover stood up.

"About time," he said.

He looked at Billie Jean as he shook off the German dust.

"Our little secret, yeah?"

"OK," said Billie Jean.

"Woof," said Rover.

And Kayla and Victoria told Billie Jean all about it.

"Who are you."

"Batteries included."

"Who are you."

"Batteries included."

"Oh my God," said Billie Jean.

"Who are you."

"Batteries, batteries, batteries."

"Who are you-ooooooo!"

"Oh my –"

"Included, included."

"God."

"Included."

"He's in prison?" asked Billie Jean.

"A guest of the nation," said Rover.

"But how will we get home? I'm exhausted."

"Don't look at me, missis," said Rover.

Meanwhile, Mister Mack followed

the boys as they crawled back through
the tunnel.

Meanwhile, the orphan catcher had
muck in her eyes. She rubbed them
and saw a boy's face right in front of
her. She screamed, and heard a voice.

"Back! Back!"
A boy's voice.
"Ha ha," she said. "Got you."

Meanwhile, a boy called Klaus was
feeling happy as he walked past
Rover, the girls and Billie Jean. He had
two shoes, and was looking forward to
his dinner.

He heard the accents. He stopped walking.

"You are Irish?" he asked.

"Who are you?" said Kayla.

"I love Ireland," said Klaus. "Especially much I like your Irish muuu-zic."

And he started singing.

"TIM REILLY WAS A HANDSOME LAD, WHO LOVED TO JUMP AND CLIMB —"

Klaus kept singing.

WARNING:

Irish music is a killer and should be approached very carefully. Always wear rubber gloves when close to Irish music. Never turn your back on Irish music and never, ever listen to it. Back to the story.

"AND HE DIED FOR DEAR OLD IRELAND TWENTY-SEVEN TIMES."

Billie Jean screamed. She grabbed Kayla, Victoria and Rover and she ran. She had to get away from the Irish music.

Rover put his paws around Billie Jean's neck and held on tight.

"I could get used to this," said Rover.

Meanwhile, Mister Mack climbed back into his cell. The boys followed him. They put the tile over the hole.

Meanwhile, Billie Jean ran through Cologne, with two girls and a dog on her back. She was slowing down, but

she could see the other woman just ahead of her.

"We're Irish!" she shouted.

A man stopped walking.

"Irish?" he said. "Oh, I love the Irish muuuu-zic."

And he started to sing.

"ME NAME IS PATSY GRADY –

AND I WORK FOR MICROSOFT –"

Billie Jean screamed, and ran past the other woman.

"Keep in touch," said Rover. "Head west," he told Billie Jean. "I know a shortcut."

"We're Irish," roared Billie Jean.

"Irish?" said another man. "We love very much the Irish muuu-zic."

He sang.

"WALT DISNEY WAS AN IRISH LAD –

HE CAME FROM BALLYMUCK –"

And Billie Jean ran.

"HE WALKED ALL DAY,

TO AMERICAY –

WITH HIS GOOD FRIEND, DÓNAL DUCK."

Meanwhile, the orphan catcher bashed her head on the tile.

And meanwhile, Rover put on his glasses, then pointed to a tree.

"Over there."

"I'm exhausted," said Billie Jean. "I need a rest."

And the dog sang.

"I'VE BEEN A WILD ROVER FOR MANY A

YEAR-RRRR –

AND I SPENT ALL MY MONEY ON

WHISKEY AND BEE-EEER –"

He sang right into Billie Jean's ear. She dashed to the tree and jumped down the hole behind it.

Meanwhile, Not-Nice opened the cell door. He stared at Robbie and Jimmy.

"Who are you?"

The floor tile rose slowly, with the orphan catcher's mucky head right under it.

"Who are you?"

"Who are you?"

And Nice walked into the cell.

"Who are you?"

"Who are you?"

"Who are you?"

"How long now?" asked Billie Jean.

"Who are you," said Kayla.

"AND IT'S NO – NAY – NEVER-RRRR –

NO – NAY – NEVER NO MORE-

RRRRRRRRRR –"

Billie Jean charged through the darkness.

The orphan catcher grabbed Jimmy and Robbie. She held their ankles and pulled them towards the hole.

"WILL I –

PLAY-YYYYYY

THE WILD ROVER-RRRRRRRR –"

Mister Mack grabbed the boys' hands.
"Who are you?" he shouted.
"Who are you?" the orphan catcher shouted back.
Billie Jean reached the end of the tunnel –
"Ouch!"
And she burst through the wall of the cell.

"NO – NEVERRRRRRR
NO – woof."

Rover stopped singing when he saw the cops.
"Who are you?" said Kayla.

"Who are you?" said Not-Nice.

"Who are you?" said Billie Jean.

"Who are you?" said the orphan catcher.

"Who *are* you?" said Billie Jean.

"I'm the bank manager's sister," said the orphan catcher. "I mean, I'm the orphan catcher."

"Let go of my children," said Billie Jean.

"No," said the orphan catcher.

"I'm their mother, that's their father. That makes them not-orphans."

"I don't care," said the orphan catcher. "I found them first."

"Let go," said Billie Jean.

"No."

"Let go," said Mister Mack.

"No."

"Let go!" said Robbie and Jimmy.

"Uh-uh," said the orphan catcher.

Kayla jumped off Billie Jean's back and walked over to the orphan catcher. She got down on her little knees and she looked straight into the orphan catcher's eyes.

And she spoke.

"Who are you."

And she head-butted the orphan catcher.

Really?

No, she didn't. And Noodles just walked under a bus.

I forgot. Sorry!

Noodles walked into the cell.

"Are yis having a sing-song?" he said.

Good old Noodles. He loves a sing-song.

No one was singing, so Noodles walked back out.

Kayla looked straight into the orphan catcher's eyes.

"Who are you."

"That's better," said the orphan catcher.

She let go of the ankles and, slowly, slowly, her head dropped down. The tile clicked back into place.

Here is what Kayla actually said: "Let go, *please*."

The orphan catcher's mucky head popped back up again.

"Good manners cost nothing," she said, and the head dropped under the tile again. "Bye-bye."

And now, Billie Jean smiled at Mister Mack.

"What kept you?" said Mister Mack.

Billie Jean went to the door and slammed it.

"I missed you," she said.

She spoke to Nice and Not-Nice.

"Who are youse?"

"We're well-known detectives," said Not-Nice. "And you're under arrest."

He felt a sharp pain in his knee. It was Victoria, and she'd just bitten him.

"Batteries *not* included," she said.

"OK, OK," said Not-Nice. "You're

not under arrest."

"Thank you," said Billie Jean. "But why have you arrested my all-time favourite husband?"

"Well," said Nice. (Not-Nice was afraid to speak. There was a little girl staring at his knee.) "He tried to rob the bank."

"He didn't," said Billie Jean. "He was trying to get a loan."

"Really?" said Nice. "That's wonderful. But what about the gun?"

"Not a gun," said Billie Jean. "A saw."

"But it looks very like a gun."

"So what?" said Jimmy. "You look very like an eejit."

"I get your point," said Nice, who knew he looked like an eejit and wasn't a bit insulted. "But one last thing," he said.

He spoke to Billie Jean.

"What about you?"

"What about me?"

"Were you, by any chance, hiding away, waiting for Mister Mack here to join you with the loot?"

"No, I wasn't," said Billie Jean.

"Oh, good," said Nice. "But where were you?"

And Billie Jean smiled.

"My name is Billie Jean Fleetwood-Mack, and I just went around the world without telling anyone. And now I claim the record."

"Congratulations," said Nice.

"Batteries included," Victoria growled at Not-Nice's knee.

"Congratulations!" said Not-Nice.

CHAPTER TWENTY-FOUR

THE DAILY OUTRAGE
OUR HEROES COME HOME,

writes Our Special Correspondent,

Paddy Hackery.

There was dancing in the streets last night as superheroes Billie Jean Fleetwood-Mack and her husband, Mister, returned to their house in – ouch!

Paddy Hackery was bitten on the knee by a little girl.

And that, really, is the end of the story.

Mister Mack went back to inventing. He invented a clever device for helping prisoners escape from prison. (Hint: it looked very like a key.) And he was inventing a tunnel digger for Robbie and Jimmy when he got a phone call. It was Mister Kimberley, his old boss at the biscuit factory.

"It's good news, Mister Mack," said Mister Kimberley. "The people of Ireland aren't interested in keeping fit any more."

"Oh good," said Mister Mack.

"They're eating biscuits again."

"Oh great," said Mister Mack.

"So we're opening the factory again."

"Oh wonderful," said Mister Mack.

"Will you come back to us, Mister Mack?"

"I'm on my way," said Mister Mack. "Hang on, though. What about the cream crackers?"

"They're too healthy and useless," said Mister Kimberley. "No one wants them. They're gone."

"Yippee!" said Mister Mack.

He threw the phone into the air.

"We'll be back," said the cream cracker in Mister Mack's head, the one that always spoiled his daydreams. "Isn't that interesting?"

But Mister Mack wasn't listening. He was looking for his shoes. He was on his way to work. He could already taste the figs and chocolate.

"I'm a working man again!" he shouted as he ran to the door.

"You've always worked for me," said Billie Jean.

She kissed him as he ran past her, out the door.

Billie Jean was a working woman. She was a Dublin firefighter, fighting factory fires and forest fires and house fires, saving lots of people and trees.

"It's a bit boring," she said. "But I like the quiet life."

Billie Jean had broken all the records she'd ever wanted — the first woman to put out a forest fire without using water. So she started training Kayla. Youngest girl to swim the English Channel. Youngest girl to run across the Sahara. They even persuaded Mister Mack to come with them now and again. Youngest girl to climb Everest carrying her father on her back.

Robbie and Jimmy had enjoyed their tunnel digging and it became their hobby, after school. They tunnelled into shops and put men's clothes in the women's department and women's clothes in the men's department. They put fat men's underpants in the babies' department and nappies in the frozen food. They tunnelled into other tunnels, until Dublin was on top of one huge tunnel. A dog called Noodles started to sing –

"IT'S
SUCH A PER-FECT DAY-YYYY –"

And Dublin collapsed into the tunnel.

Victoria also became a record breaker. Her adventures had left her with a love of falling through the air, and that was what she did for the rest of her life. She also became a surgeon. And, once, she performed a heart transplant just seconds after herself and the patient jumped out of a plane. By the time they landed, the patient had a brand-new heart. He landed on a bed in the middle of a field, and the old heart landed in a swimming pool, in the middle of the hundred-metre freestyle.

The orphan catcher also had a

change of heart. She decided that orphan catching wasn't very nice, just after the Gigglers made her walk into the you-know-what. So, she started catching butterflies instead. But she wasn't very good at that either.

"I am not a butterfly, madam. I am a vegetarian rat."

Nice and Not-Nice changed too. They still worked as a team, but Nice became less nice, and Not-Nice became much nicer. Five months after they'd arrested Mister Mack, they became the exact same, for five minutes. They were known as the Twins, but only for ten minutes.

And the Gigglers got both of them. Just at the end of the ten minutes, the Not-Nice Twins were running down the street, chasing kids who'd done nothing except belch when they were walking past the Garda station. The kids turned a corner, and the Twins turned the corner and stepped on to twin poos, put there by the Gigglers and delivered by Rover and his nephew, a mad young hound called Darren.

Rover retired. Kind of. As the kids got older, he became less interested in their adventures.

"Oh no! I've got spots on my chin. Rover, help!"

"Grow a beard, pal."

"I'm a girl."

"Walk around backwards till the spots go."

He could sort out most of their problems without standing up. But, now and again, a real adventure came his way.

"Oh no, there's a meteorite heading towards Earth. That means I'll only be able to wear my new trainers once before we die."

"How long have we got till the meteorite hits?"

"Two hours."

"No sweat."

He still sold his poo to the Gigglers – they couldn't depend on young Darren – and he became even richer. He was the first dog to own a football club when he bought Manchester United. And Manchester United became the first club to win the F.A. Cup with a poodle in goal. The poodle was female, and her name was Amanda.

Klaus kept losing shoes. But then he lost a leg as well, and all his troubles were over. He recorded a CD of Irish songs, and a duet with Sinéad O'Connor: "One Love, Two Voices, Three Legs." The slugs never tried to take over the world again, but they did take over a cabbage in a field near the Macks' house. And what about the budgies? They opened a new pet shop and they made a fortune selling the people who came into the shop to the rabbits who were already in the shop. All over Dublin, people went about their daily lives, but only because their pet rabbits let them.

"A rabbit is a burrowing animal with long ears and a fluffy tail. Isn't that interesting?"

OH NO! THE MESSAGES!

All good stories have messages, and this story has none. But here are a few anyway.

1. If you work in a bank and a man walks in with something that looks like a machine gun, it might really be a machine gun. If he says, "Give me all the cash," it probably *is* a machine gun. If, however, he says, "I'm here to fix the shelves," it is probably a saw.

2. If you ever meet a dog called Noodles, get him to sing "Bohemian Rhapsody". He'll do it for nothing, and he's brilliant.

3. The next time your father's in jail, make sure he gives you the car keys before he's locked up.

4. If you are a nice detective, you shouldn't smoke. It's bad for you, and prisoners will escape, using the matches that you drop on the floor.

5. If you ever perform a heart

transplant in mid-air, make sure you bring a flask, because you'll probably want a cup of coffee about halfway through the operation.

6. The next time you're feeding your rabbit, look into his or her big eyes and ask yourself: "Is this my rabbit, or am I this rabbit's human?"

7. If you are allergic to Irish music, stay well away from Germany. France and South Africa are safe, but be careful in Sweden, and Irish music of the most vicious kind has been known to hide in the bushes and pubs of Boston.

8. If an orphan catcher is grabbing your ankle, if a lion is about to bite your bum, if an angry bus is about to run over your head, always remember to say, "Please." It's a magic little word and it might just save your life.

THE END

Hey, pal.

There's a little word missing, Rover.

Hey, pal, *please*.

Oh, yes. Sorry, Rover. I nearly forgot.

9. If you're a poodle and your name is Amanda, Rover says, "Keep your football boots polished, Baby. Your big day is coming."

THE END

Turn the page to find out more
about Roddy Doyle and
THE GIGGLER TREATMENT. . .

An Interview with Roddy Doyle

Why did you decide to write a children's book?

I wanted to see if I could do it. I admire good children's books; I love reading them to my own children. After years of reading other writers' books, I decided to see if I could write a book of my own to read to my children.

How did you get the idea for THE GIGGLER TREATMENT?

A walk from my house to the local shops involves constant side-stepping and slaloming, constant vigilance – a straight line route is impossible because of the dog poo that festoons the footpath. I decided to turn this smelly negative into a positive, and to celebrate the sheer volume of poo on Dublin's streets.

How long did it take to write this book?

Not very long. Perhaps a month. I spent an hour at the end of each working day writing it.

Did you approach writing THE GIGGLER TREATMENT differently to your adult books?

Yes. I wrote a page or so a day, then read it to my children, to get their reactions. Then, the next day, I'd re-write and then write more and, again, read it to my children and, again, make adjustments – put back things they missed, take out things they didn't like. It became part of our after-school routine for a while. They were my editors.

How did you come up with the characters in the book? Are any of them based on people you know in real life?

Like all the characters I've ever invented, they came out of my head. The seagull, however, is based on an old school teacher and I used to go drinking with the cream crackers.

Do you have a favourite part in the book?

I think I like the first time we meet Rover best. It still makes me laugh. I enjoyed inventing him. I like the way his head works.

Do you think your view of the world has changed now compared to when you were a child?

Of course. When I was a child the world was flat. Now, it's round. When I was a child we had a black and white T.V. Now we have colour. When I was a kid I wouldn't eat sardines. Now I love them.

What books and authors did you read as a kid? Which are your biggest influences?

I read a lot when I was a child but I don't remember many authors. I loved the WILLIAM books, by Richmal Crompton. I read everything by Enid Blyton. There was a book by Edwin O'Connor, called BENJY, which I loved. It was sent to me by an uncle who worked in the US. It was probably my favourite children's book. I'm not sure about influences. They seem to vary from book to book. The shape and pace of THE GIGGLER TREATMENT are, to an extent, inspired by the Captain Underpants books. But, also, Monty Python had an influence.

What advice would you give to young writers today?

Allow the writing to become part of your day. Get into the habit. Accumulate pages of your work. Give yourself time - time is a great editor. Don't judge your work until you have put it aside for a reasonable length of time.

What do you like best about writing a book for children?

Just that - it is aimed at children. Virtually all of my other work has been for adults. All the movies I've scripted, for example, have been graded Over 15. It's nice to be able to read something of my own to my kids, and not have to wait until they are old enough to read my other work.

If you were not writing, what might you be doing instead?

I was a school teacher for 14 years. I'd probably still be doing that.